The Twilight of Magic

The Twilight of Magic

HUGH LOFTING

illustrated by Tatsuro Kiuchi

SIMON & SCHUSTER BOOKS FOR YOUNG READERS
Published by Simon & Schuster
New York   London   Toronto   Sydney   Tokyo   Singapore

SIMON & SCHUSTER BOOKS FOR YOUNG READERS
Simon & Schuster Building, Rockefeller Center
1230 Avenue of the Americas, New York, New York 10020
Text copyright 1930 by Hugh Lofting
Copyright © renewed 1958 by Josephine Lofting
Illustrations copyright © 1993 by Tatsuro Kiuchi
All rights reserved including the right of reproduction
in whole or in part in any form.
SIMON & SCHUSTER BOOKS FOR YOUNG READERS
is a trademark of Simon & Schuster.
The text of this book is set in Palatino.
Manufactured in the United States of America

10   9   8   7   6   5   4   3   2   1

Library of Congress Cataloging-in-Publication Data
Lofting, Hugh, 1886–1947.
The twilight of magic / by Hugh Lofting ;
illustrated by Tatsuro Kiuchi.
p.   cm.
Summary: In the days when magic was on the wane,
a little boy in possession of a magic whispering shell
does a service for his young king.
[1. Magic—Fiction.   2. Middle Ages—Fiction.]
I. Kiuchi, Tatsuro, ill.   II. Title.
PZ7.L827Tw   1993   [Fic]—dc20   92–15766   CIP
ISBN: 0–671–78358–0

FOREWORD

Exactly why my father decided to interrupt the flow of the Doctor Dolittle series to write *The Twilight of Magic* in 1930 is not quite clear. Although both are fantasies, they differ considerably in form and content.

The Twilight of Magic is classical fantasy, dealing with the workings of magic, which no one would be so presumptuous or pedantic as to try to explain in scientific terms. Because the characters and the medieval setting come truly alive, in detail, the supernatural powers of Agnes the Applewoman and her whispering shell are accepted unquestionably within the context of the story.

Doctor Dolittle is fantasy in the same sense as good science fiction: It is probable fiction containing a minimum of improbabilities and based on scientifically sound principles. Here, if the reader can accept the premise that Polynesia, the Doctor's pet parrot, can speak and understand English, it seems reasonable that she could also teach animal language to Doctor Dolittle. Yet *The Twilight of Magic* has one main factor in common with Doctor Dolittle—that same universal appeal which transcends the limitations of children's fantasies. My father had the ability to draw his young audience into the center of the adventure rather than relegating them to the position of being mere spectators on the sidelines. The reader saw the adult world of Hugh Lofting through the eyes of Tommy Stubbins in Doctor Dolittle and Giles and Anne in *The Twilight of Magic*. The author's intrinsic belief in and respect for children's values was detected. The absence of a condescending tone, which marks so many attempts at juvenile literature, was noticed and appreciated.

As a child I had no particular understanding or sympathy for the arts and writing as a profession. I was not particularly impressed by the fact that my father was an author. So I believe I am making an objective evaluation when I say that *The Twilight of Magic* was one of my all-time favorites. Needless to say, I was very pleased when Simon & Schuster decided to reissue this delightful story. I hope you enjoy it as much as I do.

Christopher Lofting

CONTENTS

Book I

BOOK II

The Twilight of Magic

BOOK I

CHAPTER ONE

GILES AND ANNE

One evening long ago two children lay in bed in an attic. From downstairs the noise of rattling knives and forks came up to them. And the children, as they often did, were guessing what guests their mother and father had invited for supper. They knew most of their parents' friends by name and sight, but they themselves were not yet old enough to be allowed to take supper with the grown-ups—except at Christmas time and on birthdays. For in those times life was much stricter for young people than it is now. The boy's name was Giles. The girl's name was Anne. They were twins, nine years old.

They could hear, too, the tinkle of the bell which their father rang when he wanted the serving maid to come in and change the plates. It was fun to try and tell from the smells of the food, and from the noises of glasses, china, and silver, which dishes were being served.

"They are having the pudding now," whispered

Anne. "Didn't you hear that oven door slam just then, Giles?"

"Sh!" growled the boy. "Not so loud—with our own door open and all. We're supposed to be asleep. No, they've finished the pudding. I can hear Father cracking nuts—or else it is that grumpy old Dr. Seymour. His voice is hard to mistake. Besides, I heard Mother say something about his coming tonight."

"How late the light lasts!" said Anne. "How can they expect us to sleep while the setting sun still glows on the windowpane?"

"And how hot it is!" said Giles, throwing back a blanket from his bed. "I'm going to open that other window. One is not enough on a night like this."

He stepped quietly out of bed and, moving over to the dormer, gently opened the latch and swung the casement outward. He gazed down into the street. Hardly anyone was abroad. The town clock chimed the half hour—half past seven. On the tiles of the opposite roof a black cat stretched himself lazily in the last of the red sunlight.

"Listen, Anne," whispered the boy. "Come over here—but quiet now."

"What is it?" asked his sister. Noiselessly she glided from her bed and across the floor to his side.

"It's the Applewoman," said Giles. "Don't you hear her? She's away down the street around the corner. Soon you'll see her."

"I don't hear anything," said Anne. "Only the cracking of the nuts downstairs. I wish I had some. It makes me hungry to listen to them."

"Stop talking," said her brother, "and then you'll hear her. A long way off. But you can catch it. 'Apples! Fine pippins for sale!' It's what she always cries."

"The Applewoman!" said little Anne thoughtfully. "I wonder why grown-up people don't seem to like her, Giles. Do you know?"

"Oh, pshaw!" said her brother. "I don't believe they know themselves. They don't understand her, I reckon. People are nearly always afraid of what they can't understand—except the very brave ones, maybe. I never could see anything wrong with the Applewoman—though it's true I've never spoken to her. 'Shragga the Witch'! What a name to call her! But have you noticed it is only the grown-ups who call her that? To the children she is always just 'Agnes the Applewoman.' I don't believe that woman ever did a bad deed in her whole life—for all her ugly looks."

"Shragga the Witch!" murmured Anne. "It is indeed a terrible name to fasten upon anyone. Yet she is queer, Giles. Do you know what Mary Seymour says about her? She says she's a mind reader."

"What on earth is that?" asked Giles.

"She can read a person's thoughts—or so Mary says. She can tell what you're thinking about without your saying a word."

"Oh, I don't believe that," said Giles. "Maybe she just guesses—and guesses right."

"But if she guesses right all the time," said Anne, "it would be the same as doing it, wouldn't it?"

"Humph!" her brother muttered. "I'd like to see her do it. I think of a whole lot of things in one day. It would be very hard to guess *my* thoughts."

"Listen, she's nearer now," whispered Anne. "She must be just around the bend. Goodness! I wish that noise of clattering plates would give over for a moment down below!"

"Yes," said Giles. "But anyhow we'll see her in a second or— Goodness, Anne! *Look at the cat!*"

On the roof opposite, the black cat was indeed behaving strangely. Still glowing with the rosy light of the evening sun, he was now bounding up and down in the queerest way, while the long flat shadows behind him leapt still more wildly on the sloping tiles.

"He sees her," whispered Anne. "He can see around the bend from here, while we can't. . . . Oh, Giles, let's go back to bed! I'm afraid. Don't let Agnes see us here! Maybe the grown-ups are right, Giles. Maybe . . . maybe she *is* a witch!"

CHAPTER TWO

SHRAGGA THE WITCH

For a moment or two Giles did not answer. Very still he stayed at the window, frowning across the street. The cat's antics seemed now to have become almost a mad jumping dance, growing wilder and wilder as the singing voice of the woman drew nearer.

"Apples! Apples! Fine pippins for sale!"

And then at last the children saw her. The cracking of nuts could still be heard from the parents' table on the ground floor. The children for a while were silent. Seeing the old woman was more important than talking. She had a long, very wrinkled face—a clever face, a wise one—but not unkind. She pushed her apple barrow before her with strong even shoves, stopping once in a while to raise her hand to the side of her mouth while she made her call: *"Apples!"*

"I don't believe it," repeated Giles. "Reading people's thoughts! If *she* could do it, why couldn't anyone? If I stuck my head under a pillow, could you tell me what I was thinking?"

"Of course I couldn't," Anne whispered. "But that is what Mary Seymour said: All Agnes has to do is to look at you and she knows what is passing through your mind."

"Apples! Apples! Fine pippins for sale!"

The old woman's voice rang out nearer and louder. She still stared straight ahead of her along the street, looking neither to the right of her nor to the left. At last she stopped beneath the children's window, seemingly tired of crying to an almost empty street.

Anne craned her neck out through the casement.

"Oh, Giles; what beautiful apples! I'm hungry."

Giles smacked his lips and grunted, "Umph, look at that enormous red one, almost at the end of her barrow, Anne. I'd like that one, wouldn't you? Um . . . my!"

And then for the first time, suddenly, Agnes the Applewoman looked up, straight at the children's window. A kind and almost beautiful smile spread over her funny old wrinkled face. Without turning her eyes aside she reached out and grasped an apple and with a queer quick twist of the wrist threw it straight up into the dormer window. It landed gently in Giles's hands.

"It's the very one," whispered the boy. "The red one I chose!"

"Apples! Apples! Fine pippins for sale!" On went the Applewoman, on went the barrow.

The cat had disappeared from the roof; and as Agnes passed out of sight around the bend of the street, they saw the animal following at her heels.

"Apples! Apples! Fine pippins for sale!" The voice was now soft and distant.

"Oh, my goodness, Giles!" Anne's face was quite pale as she turned to her brother and pointed to the rosy fruit lying in his hands. "The woman picked out the very apple you were longing for—the one you were already chewing in your mind. And she couldn't possibly have heard a word you whispered. If that isn't reading people's minds, I'd like to know what is. Do you believe it now?"

CHAPTER THREE

LUKE

The apple had been divided and eaten. It was now past midnight, and yet the children were not asleep. Dr. Seymour's deep voice mumbled on downstairs. And still Giles was arguing in whispers that what they had seen had been nothing more than a happy accident; and still Anne stuck to it that Agnes's thought reading had been clearly proved.

And so it was two very weary-eyed children who came down to breakfast next morning. But they were at the table before their parents. When their father appeared, it was Giles who first noticed that he wore a worried look. This later troubled Anne also; but in those days children were supposed to be seen and not heard, so she did not speak of it then. And as soon as the meal was over, the youngsters went out into the garden.

"What do you think is the matter with Father, Giles?" asked Anne when they were well away from the house.

"I'm not quite certain," said Giles. "But after you fell asleep last night, I crept down the stairs a little way. And from what I heard I believe Father owes Dr. Seymour—and others too—a lot of money. I had thought that Father had money enough for his needs, but it seems he has been borrowing from the doctor and the doctor wants him now to pay it back."

"Is it very much?" asked Anne.

"Yes," said Giles seriously. "I imagine it would be very much more than he could pay now. And Dr. Seymour was almost rude. He must have it within the week, he said—needs it to pay his own bills. Then a long talk followed, Father saying he couldn't possibly pay it in so short a time and the doctor almost shouting he must have it. This money business seems a curse. I wish people could live without it altogether."

"Dear me!" said Anne thoughtfully. "I wonder . . . if anyone . . . maybe Agnes the Applewoman could do something. Couldn't we go and see her, Giles?"

"My goodness, Anne, don't you know that all the grown-up people would make no end of fuss? You know they call her a witch. What help could she give us?"

"Who can tell?" said Anne. "But you said yourself you had faith in that old woman. And I am beginning to feel the same way too. Though I don't quite know why. Maybe it's her kindly smile, or the way the animals follow her about. Grown-up people sometimes get very set in their ways. Let's go and see her, Giles. She will do us no harm, of that I am sure."

So a little later Giles and Anne stepped out through the lower garden gate behind their father's home and started to make a tour of the town.

They inquired of the old blind man, who sat in front of Our Lady's Church, where they could find Agnes the Applewoman.

"You mean Shragga the Witch?" said he gruffly, his whole body bristling with suspicion.

"All right," said Giles, "if you would call her so. Where does she live?"

"I . . . don't know," said the blind man, and he made the sign of the cross.

The children wandered on, looking here and there for someone else to ask, till finally they came upon a lame boy, a town character whom they had known almost as long as they could remember. He did not seem nearly so closemouthed and careful.

"Agnes," said he. "Why, of course I know where she lives. You go down to the bridge crossing the South River. And at the foot of the Archers' Tower, you'll find a path running along the edge of the stream. Follow that till you see a little hut set up high, where the tides cannot reach. And that's where Agnes lives. A fine woman. You'll like meeting her. Who cares if the Mayor and all those stuffy aldermen call her a witch? There are some who know her for what she is."

CHAPTER FOUR

THE HUT BY THE RIVER

The children thanked the lame boy and went on. By following his directions carefully they at length came in sight of the hut he had spoken of. It was very small and shabby and looked as though it had sunk down from sheer age and feebleness into the mud that surrounded the tower. Many people might have passed it by without seeing it. It was only after a scramble over the half-dried ooze of the river that Giles and Anne could reach it.

The door was shut tight. There were no signs of life anywhere. Giles crept up and knocked timidly. There was no answer.

"Maybe she's away," whispered Anne.

"Wait a moment," said Giles. And he rapped upon the door again, more loudly.

"Come in," called a voice gently.

The boy took his sister's hand in his, lifted the latch, and pushed firmly. A square black hole opened before him. There seemed at first to be no light inside the hut whatever. It took a little courage to enter. And Anne felt her brother's hand tighten on her own. He led her forward and downward into the darkness, feeling ahead for stairs with his feet.

"Why, I declare!" said the gentle voice again. "It's my apple children. Come in, come in. Can you see? Wait, now. We will make a light."

There was the sound of a scratching of a tinderbox. At the same time the door snapped to and latched itself behind them, though neither Giles nor Anne could make out by what means it closed. It was darker now than ever. But presently a flame glowed up, and they saw the old woman bending over a table, lighting a candle.

"I am glad to see you," she said, a smile spreading over her wrinkled face. "A little light makes it more cheerful, eh? And a fire— Oh, goodness me! Look, it's gone out. What a welcome! No light and no fire—with a cold wind blowing and all. Just a minute. Sit down and we'll soon get it going."

The old woman took up a bellows and with its point stirred the gray ashes in the hearth. Then, as she started to blow, two big black cats came forward out of the gloom carrying sticks in their mouths. Agnes took the sticks from them and fed the red coals, now glowing into life among the swirling dust. The cats kept going backward and forward for more wood in a most businesslike way, as though they were quite used to helping with the housework in this fashion. Soon a merry little blaze was flaring up the chimney. Its light helped the meager candle on the table and made the small room less gloomy and strange.

"Ha!" said Agnes, standing back. "That's better. Now, let me see what fruit we have to eat. Sit down, children. Draw that bench up here—so."

Then she rummaged down into the back of the hut and brought forward a large pear and two luscious peaches. The youngsters took them from her outstretched hands and murmured awkward thanks. Agnes seated herself on the bench between them.

"Dear, dear!" she said. "It isn't often I have visitors— except the kind I do not want. Now, tell me: What can I do for you, little people?"

"Well—er—er," Giles began. "We—er—thought perhaps—" Then he stopped, silent.

"Humph!" muttered Agnes as the two black cats crept forward again and rubbed their heads against her knee. "Perhaps the little girl can tell me better."

"Well, you see, Mother Agnes," said Anne, fidgeting restlessly on the bench, "you—er—er—"

The old woman looked steadily at her as she hesitated. Then she took Anne's small hand in hers a moment.

"Is it something about your father, child?" she asked presently.

At that both children jumped a little and looked at

each other. Anne was on the point of asking the old woman how she knew. But she found her still staring steadily at her and went on: "Yes, it is. He's in trouble."

"In what way?" asked Agnes. "Business? Money matters, my dear?"

"Oh, Mother Agnes," said Anne, "he always has had enough for the needs of his whole family. And now, suddenly, he seems to be in debt. His life is troubled. He looks worried, sometimes almost ill. . . ."

"Well?" asked the Applewoman gently after a moment.

Anne again glanced across at her brother, this time as if for help.

"We thought we ought to do something to try to aid him," Giles put in. "That's why we came to you."

"To me?" said Agnes. "Well, well! And did you tell anyone you were coming?"

The children shook their heads.

"This needs thinking over," said Agnes, more, it seemed, to herself than to anyone else. She got up and moved over again to the back of the hut, where she disappeared behind a ragged curtain. The two cats rose also, like pages waiting on a queen, and followed her. At once the children slid together on the bench. And Anne whispered: "What do you think of her, Giles?"

"I think she's fine," her brother whispered back. "But those cats? My, they're strange!"

"Did you notice the way she seemed to know what

you were going to say before you say it?" asked Anne.

"Yes," answered Giles. "But you're not afraid of that, are you?"

"Oh, no. I ought to be, I suppose, if it's magic. But somehow I don't seem to be. I like her—a lot. What a funny, queer little room, Giles, isn't it?" Anne's glance swept around the inside of the hut as she bit into a ripe peach. "Copper saucepans on the walls. No pictures. Old wooden chests—I wonder what's inside them. A sleeping-basket for the cats—I suppose they make their own beds. And the apple barrow over there, see the wheels sticking out from under the cover full of patches. Old clothes and a bonnet hanging on the peg. Oh, I do hope she'll be able to help us about Father's troubles, Giles. But she seems dreadfully poor herself. . . . Sh! Here she comes back again."

Agnes hobbled forward to the bench at the fire. The two cats followed her into the room. Then they went off into a far corner, sat down side by side like a pair of soldiers, and watched the blaze from a distance.

"Well, now, young people," said the Applewoman, "are you aware that you might get into serious trouble if your parents learned that you had been here?"

"Yes, surely," said Anne. "But, oh, it's so important that something be done for Father, Mother Agnes. And you were the only one we could think of who might be able to help."

"I see, I see," muttered the old woman. "You know

what folks call me, I suppose?" she asked, suddenly looking at Giles with black eyes wide open, piercing.

"Shragga the Witch," murmured the boy in almost a whisper, not meeting her gaze.

"That's it. 'Shragga the Witch.'" She nodded. "A lot they know, the fools! Tell me, do I look like a witch to you?"

"No, indeed," said Giles quickly. "You look to me like a very—er—sensible woman. But we can't quite understand those cats. That one over there, now, he has a sort of queer creepy look in his eyes when he stares at me. Seems almost as though he were listening, taking in everything that's said."

Agnes chuckled.

"Would you like him to come over here and join us by the fire? . . . All right. Here he comes, look."

The big sleek creature, with the firelight glinting green in his eyes, stalked slowly across the floor and planted himself solemnly at Giles's feet.

"But there you are!" cried the boy. "You didn't call him, you gave him no order, and yet he came as soon as you wanted him. How do you do it?"

"You mean, how does he do it?" said Agnes. "Well, I'm not sure that I know myself. They are a pair of ordinary cats to look at, as you see. Larger than most—but very much cleverer. They were born twins, kittens from the same litter, you know. Perhaps it's because we have lived together so long. They are older than either of you. And they are both very fond of me—quite jealous about it sometimes, it would seem. Though, strange to say, they never fight and have never cried or made a single sound since I've had them. When they were younger, I used to teach them all manner of tricks. It was very easy with such clever creatures. But now they seem to teach themselves—or each other. Sometimes I fancy that they are continually on the watch to know, or guess at, what I want, what I am going to do next. And that seems to sharpen up their wits. For anyone can see that they watch each other as well as watching me. But, be that as it may, they certainly often carry out my wishes without being told. And, after all, what's strange about that? The same thing happens with people. But we are getting away from your father and his troubles."

"You will be able to help, yes?" asked Anne eagerly.

"Well, now," said Agnes, "wait a minute. First of all, I want you children to have one or two things quite clear in your minds. Since I am called a witch, I am in daily danger of being hauled up before the magistrates and perhaps even of being burned for my sins."

Both the cats suddenly sprang onto her lap together. Anne fancied that one looked fierce and the other looked sad. Agnes smiled, patted them, and pushed them gently down.

"Therefore," she went on, "it is necessary that we go about the matter with much care. For there may be danger in it—for you and others. I don't want you to tell any lies, to your parents or anyone else. But for the present I want you to keep your little mouths shut very tight."

Both the children tried to close their jaws at once. But as Anne's mouth was full of peach, and her brother's full of pear, they only succeeded in looking like two bad cases of toothache. Agnes laughed.

"I only meant that you mustn't talk. No one knows you came here—"

"Oh, excuse me," Giles interrupted. "We did ask two people how to find your home: Michael the Blind Man and Luke."

"That's no matter of consequence," said Agnes. "Old Michael is no gossip, and he doesn't know whether you got here or no. As for Luke, he is a good boy. I've been trying to set that twisted joint in his leg. You can talk to him as much as you want. But your parents don't know you have been here. And no one else must know. Remember, now. And don't let yourselves get into a position where you'll be questioned. And try"—Agnes rose from the bench and placed a hand on the shoulder of each—"try not to ask *me* too many questions either," she ended slowly.

She moved over to the door and opened it.

"It is time for you to be going," she said. "Come back tomorrow morning and—well, we will see what can be done. Good-bye!"

CHAPTER FIVE

IN THE SEA GARDEN

Next morning the children were so anxious to get back to the Applewoman's home that they hardly ate any breakfast at all. Luckily for them their parents had not yet risen. And only the old cook Elsbeth grumbled something after them about not finishing their porridge, as they sped out of the house toward the garden gate.

The town at that early hour was very quiet, with almost empty streets. Fifteen minutes of running brought them again to the door of Agnes's hut.

This time they did not have to knock. The door swung open as they approached, and the old woman, with a bonnet on her head, came out to greet them.

"It's a good day for the seashore," said she. "Let's go down and hunt for shells and pebbles while the tide is out."

"Yes, but we won't forget about Father, will we?" asked Anne.

"Oh, no," crooned Agnes in a strange, singsong voice. "You know, I never forget anything. Often I wish I could. Come along, youngsters."

Silently the two children followed her down the funny winding streets, past wharves and landing walls, till a fresh sea wind struck their faces. It set the thrill of adventure tingling through their minds. Just the sharp clean scent of it conjured up glories of travel, voyage pictures which they had never known but which they hoped someday to see.

Soon the town was left behind entirely. And now old Mother Agnes led the way more slowly, over the loose sands of a beach.

Farther yet the shore took on a wilder look, with high cliffs, rocks, and bays. And there were pools, pools that lay upon the beach like little lakes where creatures swam or crawled, crabs and shrimps and burrowing things. They seemed so easy to catch that Anne was all for stopping to gather up some shellfish. But the Apple-woman seemed bent on going farther, as though she had a place in mind to reach.

At last when they came to it, the children found it well worth their patience and the walk. Where two walls of tumbled rocks stretched down from the cliffs into the sea, a piece of the beach was surrounded and cut off from the eyes of the world. It seemed like a fairies' sea garden. Big wet boulders, patterned with barnacles and mussels, hung with curtains of kelp, stood close together in rows and squares—a little town, in fact, of tiny streets, with something new to find around each corner. Sometimes these streets of Boulder Town turned into canals, linking together more ponds and tiny lakes where gay anemones and starfish waved beneath the water.

The children, every other thought and care swept from their minds, ran or waded to and fro from place to place, each forever calling to the other to come and see a new discovery.

So many things were to be seen, caves of mystery to be explored, colored pebble-gems to be collected and goodness knows what besides, that it must have been nearly an hour before the youngsters suddenly remembered they had not seen Agnes since they came here.

They found her, after some hunting, on the far side of a large rock. Here the tides had scoured out a pool larger and deeper than the rest, and under the overhanging boulder no bottom could be seen to its fascinating blue-green depths. It might have been the lair of some monster of story, half beast, half fish.

At the side of the pool was a piece of driftwood, a long stout timber from some wrecked ship. This Agnes was using as a seat—and as a table also, it appeared. For on it she had spread out fruits and sandwiches and cheese, a whole picnic luncheon taken from a little box which she had brought with her.

She invited the youngsters to come and eat. And it

was only after they were seated and had their mouths full of food that they found how hungry they had grown and that their weary legs were glad to rest.

And later, even after the luncheon was all gone, they sat on, well fed and contented, watching the beauty of the sky and sea and shore change with the shifting sun. Anne had noticed a number of weeds and plants which Agnes had laid out at the end of the timber to dry. And on asking about them learned that they were things the Applewoman used in the making of her medicines. From medicine the conversation turned to many different matters; and the children enjoyed their long talk with this strange new friend as much as any other part of the outing.

Anne had no idea how late it was when thoughts of her father and his troubles came again to her mind. But she did remember long afterward that at that point, when she turned to Agnes to speak, she found the old woman's keen eyes had been staring at her steadily and thoughtfully. And it was the Applewoman who spoke first.

"Did you ever listen to a shell to hear the roaring of the sea in it?" she asked.

"Oh, yes," cried Giles, breaking in. "We listened to one this morning, a pink spotted one."

"Well, they're very different, you know," said Agnes. "The size and the shape of them make them so. Some sing a high song and others a low; some loud and some soft. While there are yet others that are very peculiar indeed. Let me see, now, if I can find one and show you what I mean. If I'm lucky, I might find *the* one."

From where she sat the old woman, rolling back her sleeves, reached down into the deep pool at their feet. For a long time her hand moved and swayed beneath the water. Both children thought they saw her lips moving as though she were muttering something to herself.

"What did she mean, *the* one?" Anne whispered in her brother's ear.

"I don't know," he whispered back. "But remember what she said: not too many questions. I've an idea that something queer is going to happen."

Then both children gave a little gasp. For the heads of the two black cats had suddenly appeared, as if from nowhere, staring into the pool over the woman's shoulders. Their big green eyes followed the movements of her arm with keen expectant interest as it searched, groping in the depths.

At last very slowly Agnes's hand came to the top and in its knotted grasp was a shell. It was a beauty and like no other the children had ever seen: the size of a large apple; green on the outside, pearly white within; plump, almost round in shape, screwed slightly at one end. It was half filled with sand. Agnes rinsed it clean and then examined it carefully. And Anne heard her whisper to herself: "What luck! It *is* the one—and not a chip on it."

Then she looked up at the children and that kind

wrinkly smile spread over her face, which for a while
had worn an anxious, worried look.

"But where on earth did these cats come from, Mother
Agnes?" asked Giles.

"Oh, they just followed me out from the town most
likely," said the old woman. "Never mind them.
They're always turning up. I want you to hold this shell
to your ear now and hear how it can sing you the roaring
song of the sea."

From where they were standing hardly anything of
the ocean's surf could be seen or heard except the little
murmurous rushes of flat water that from time to time
ran in and out again over the shingly sands between the
boulders.

Giles held the shell to his ear.

"Do you hear anything?" asked Agnes.

For a moment the boy was silent, listening. But soon
a slow smile came over his screwed-up face.

"Oh, my, yes!" he murmured. "I hear great waves
breaking on the shore, rolling, fighting up against the
cliffs, tumbling and beating on the rocks. Then falling
back again with a weaker washy sound. . . . Now they
come thundering in some more. It's a storm. . . . I hear
great winds screaming through trees and the rigging
of ships. . . . And now it dies down again— Oh, my
gracious!"

Giles dropped the shell upon the sand as though it
had bitten him.

"It's hot!" he gasped. "It suddenly grew hot."

"Don't be afraid of it," said the old woman. "It did not get hot enough to hurt you really, did it? And it never will."

Without waiting for the boy to say anything more, Agnes buttoned up her cape at the throat and placed under her arm the little lunch box, which was now filled with the medicine plants. The two cats rose and moved to her side, as though they, too, were preparing to depart. Somewhat to Anne's alarm the Applewoman then stepped up the rocks a little way till she had gained a narrow footpath that led toward the top of the cliffs. Only one of the cats followed her. And as she stood there, about a man's height above their heads, the children both felt that some odd change had come over her. The wind from off the sea billowed out her cape behind her and rippled along the glossy black fur of her strange companion.

"I must leave you now, little people," she said slowly. "And it may be a long time before I see you again. Take the shell and guard it with great care from breaking. For it is very precious. And now listen, listen and remember!" Her right hand rose slowly from her side, as if to hold their attention to her words. The last of the sun suddenly disappeared into the sea, and the breeze of coming twilight blew more freshly and strong. Her voice now sounded like someone chanting, a long way off, yet clear and sharp.

"Whoever carries the Whispering Shell to the one in greatest need of it shall make his fortune. . . . I must be gone. Lest you should not find your way safely in the dark, one of my cats will remain to guide you home. Good luck to you! I will see you both again. Farewell."

With rather a sad, bewildered feeling in their hearts, the two watched her hobble up the footpath toward the high ground at the cliff tops. Presently Anne gripped her brother's arm and pointed to the other cat. He was already leading the way ahead of them down the beach. Giles picked up the shell at his feet.

And then, still too puzzled and thoughtful for talk, they both fell in behind their guide and started homeward through the twilight.

CHAPTER SIX

THE WHISPERING SHELL

The children were back in their attic. It was a little later than their usual hour for going to bed. On the way home the cat had kept them running fast, as though he knew they were not going to be in time for supper and would be blamed for their lateness. But no one except the cook had remarked on it, and they had got safely upstairs without a scolding.

"What do you make of it, Giles," Anne asked, "her going off like that and leaving us alone on the shore?"

"I've no idea," said the boy. "She had other business to attend to, I suppose. What I'm interested in is this thing she left with us."

And he drew from his pocket the big green shell and laid it gently on the table between himself and his sister.

"*Isn't* it beautiful?" said Anne. "Let me listen to it. I'd like to hear the roaring of the sea."

She took it and held it to her ear.

"Wonderful!" she said presently. "The sea could almost be pouring through the room here. It's much better than any shell I ever tried before. You can nearly smell the salt water, the flying spray. . . . Now it stops. . . . It's growing warm—hotter and hotter, Giles— Oh, will it hurt me?"

"No, no," said her brother quickly. "Hang on. For pity's sake, don't drop it! You heard Agnes say it would never grow hot enough to hurt you."

With grim determination Anne still held it to her ear. And presently a queer look came into her face.

"Why," said she breathlessly, "I hear someone talking about me. . . . It's the cook. She says I left an awful mess of crumbs beneath the table tonight. It isn't true." Anne took the shell away from her ear and scowled across the table at her brother. "Those were your crumbs, Giles. I *never* drop crumbs on the floor—at least hardly ever. . . . Oh, now it grows cold again."

"What do you mean?" said Giles, grabbing the shell from her. "You heard voices in the shell? You must be dreaming. I knew it could grow hot and cold. But voices? . . . Let me listen."

The boy held it to his own ear.

"Nothing," he said after a moment. "Nothing but the old sea roaring."

"But wait!" cried Anne. "Wait till it grows warm again. That's when *I* heard voices."

Giles brought the shell to rest upon the table.

"Hark to me, Anne," he said severely. "You don't mean to tell me you believe this shell can talk?"

"I would not have done," said Anne gently, "if I had not heard it. But the shell isn't talking itself. It's only letting you hear what other people say."

"Such rubbish!" Giles grunted. "Such rub— Ow— oo!"

He snatched his hand from off the shell.

"Don't mind if it grows warm," said Anne. "Remember what Agnes said. Listen now before it gets cold again."

Giles tried once more.

"It's Father speaking," said he presently, his voice atremble, "—talking about me."

There was a minute's silence while the boy listened and his sister waited.

"Well?" said she when at length he set the shell down. "What did he say about you?"

"Oh—er—nothing important," said the boy with a frown. "Sometimes I think Father doesn't understand me very well. He might have had a worse son. 'It's too bad that good-for-nothing boy has gone to bed,' he was saying. 'I can't find my big hammer anywhere. He would soon find it for me. The only thing Giles was ever any good for was finding things.'"

"Never mind," said Anne. "Be thankful that you're good for something. Now it's my turn, Giles. Let me listen. I think this is a splendid game, don't you?"

"Er—yes," said her brother, pushing the shell across to her. "But it depends on what you hear."

Already Anne had the shell clasped tightly to her ear.

"The sea!" she murmured. "The old sea, mumbling and tossing, hissing and washing."

And she began to hum a little tune of her own as she rocked to and fro to that song of the waves. Then suddenly she stopped. A smile spread over her face. Her eyes sparkled as she pressed the shell still closer against her ear. At last, slowly, she put it back upon the table with a deep sigh.

"Dear me!" she murmured. "Of course I always knew it myself. But I hadn't known that anyone else knew it."

"Knew what?" asked Giles in a grumpy tone.

"Somebody just said that I was the best-behaved girl in the town. I didn't recognize the voice. But it's true. So anyone might have said it."

She pushed the shell across the table to her brother.

"Your turn, Giles," she said. And she settled herself back in her chair with hands folded on her lap.

"Look here," said her brother, suddenly rising and pushing back his chair, which made a scraping sound. "Sh!" he hissed. "Blow out the candle. Someone might come up. We are supposed to be asleep. . . . So! We can go to bed by moonlight. Now let's get to the bottom of this thing. Have you noticed anything peculiar about the way the shell speaks, Anne?"

"Certainly," said his sister. "For one thing, it always grows hot first."

"Yes," said the boy. "But did you notice that when you hold it, the voices only say things about *you*; and when I hold it, they only say things about *me*. I think we have its secret now. Let's try again."

And so for hours, talking in whispers, the children sat up in their nightclothes. While one was listening to the shell, the other would listen for footsteps on the stairs, lest they should be caught at their work.

Anne heard her mother speak of her and a new frock for Easter she was making for her daughter; Giles heard his father speak again—this time of what the boy should be when he grew up; they both heard Dr. Seymour speak of them together; and each heard Luke the Lame Boy speak of them separately—apparently talking aloud to himself in his bed of straw.

As it grew later, and more and more of the townspeople put their lights out and went to bed, the shell grew warm less often. But in the end the children were sure they had proved its secret: that he who held it upon his person would feel it grow warm if anyone anywhere in the world spoke of him.

They were now both dead tired. And with the shell safely hidden beneath his pillow, Giles murmured as he fell asleep: "I suppose it's magic. . . . I s'pose it's magic. Don't you think . . . it's magic, Anne?"

But from Anne's bed there came no answer. She was already asleep.

CHAPTER SEVEN

MICHAEL THE BLIND MAN

Next morning it was only just light when Giles woke his sister up—by throwing a slipper over onto her cot.

"The thing to work out now," said Giles, "is, who is to get the shell. 'Whoever shall carry the Whispering Shell to the one in greatest need of it shall make his fortune'—that's what Agnes said. Well, Father is the one most in need. How about him?"

At once, still fuddled with sleep though she was, Anne shook her head hard.

"Be sensible, Giles," she warned. "What would Father have to do with anything like this, which smacks of magic. Fancy asking such a very—er—sensible man to carry around a shell in his pocket, waiting for it to get hot before he listened to it! No, Giles, we've got to be very careful how we go about this business. I would not be surprised if we find it very difficult to get any grown-up person even to take the shell and try it."

"Dr. Seymour, then," said Giles.

"Worse still," said Anne. "I wouldn't dare even to explain the matter to such a stuffy old grump."

"But he fancies himself a very important person," said Giles. "I should think he would want to know what people were saying about him."

"He wouldn't care to hear what *I* would be saying about him," Anne muttered. "No. He's no good to us. But why should we begin with the high and mighty? If we don't go carefully about this, we'll only have the shell taken from us and get a whole lot of trouble, maybe, in exchange. Let's begin with the poor and lowly, someone who can't do us any harm if he doesn't hold by what we're doing. Agnes didn't say the fortune would come *from* the person we take the shell to—only that a fortune would be *made*. Yet it is certain that the right person can be found. She wouldn't have given it to us just to fool us. We've got to try it out first—on many different kinds of people perhaps—and see what happens."

"The poor and lowly? Humph!" muttered Giles thoughtfully. "I have it: Michael the Blind Man."

"A good idea," said Anne. "To one who cannot see, it ought to be specially helpful. . . . Though we may have difficulty even with him. He has a suspicious nature. Well, let's try him first. Anyhow, he likes us. That's something."

So, later in the morning the children went forth into the town. Michael was one person who could always be found. At the east entrance to Our Lady's Church, he sat within the great arch—with all the saints carved around it—rain or shine, from daylight to dark. Beside him sat his faithful mongrel dog, Timothy, who barked out his thanks when folks put money in the little tin box that hung upon the blind man's chest. Every morning the dog led Michael to the church and every evening he led him home again.

He wagged his tail in welcome as he saw the children coming. The blind man heard, or felt, the dog's movements. He lifted his head to face the sky—seeking shadows.

"Good day to you, Michael," said Anne gently.

"Good morning, children," said the blind man, whose quick ears heard two pairs of footsteps.

"Listen," Anne began. "We have a shell here which we would like you to keep for a while."

"Why should I keep it?" grunted the old man.

Giles was about to burst out with a long explanation of what the shell could do, but Anne broke in: "Take it just as a favor to us, Michael," said she. "We want you to try it."

And then she explained to him in what manner the shell worked.

He scowled as she finished.

"I don't quite like it," said he. "Where did you get this thing, child?"

"Oh, don't ask me that now, Michael, please," said

Anne. "Just trust us that no harm will come to you from it. After all, you know us, don't you?"

"Oh, aye," said the old man slowly at last. "I'd trust some of you youngsters further than I'd trust your elders—and that's the truth. But I have no liking for conjuring tricks, mark you. A blind man's life is a life of puzzling anyhow. I'm loath, I suppose, to take over any new riddles. Give me your shell."

He stretched out his big white hand and Anne placed the shell upon it. It closed with that curious searching feel that the blind use to take the place of seeing.

"We will come again tomorrow or the next day," said Anne, "and learn what you have heard, Michael."

"Very good, child," said he. "I will expect you."

CHAPTER EIGHT

JOHANNES THE PHILOSOPHER

Two days later the children were back again at the
east entrance of the church.

"Well, Michael," said Anne eagerly, "what did the
shell tell you?"

"Nothing," said he. "What could you expect? No one
ever talks about me."

"But didn't it ever even grow warm?" asked Giles
with wide-open eyes.

"Oh, aye, it grew warm once," grumbled Michael.
"And when I listened to it, I heard only Timothy barking. He'd gone out after I was abed—across the river
chasing rats. Afraid he was, I reckon, that he'd not get
back in time to take me out in the morning. My own
dog barking—talking in his own language—that was all
I heard. What else could I hear, Michael, the blind beg-
gar? No one ever talks about me. . . . Here's your shell,
youngsters. Go, and my blessing with you."

Sadly the children took the shell and made their way back toward home. For a space neither of them spoke.

"Well, what do we do now?" said Giles at last. "We didn't learn much from that. It seems to me, in spite of what you say, we ought to seek some richer person. After all, if we are to make a fortune for Father by means of the shell, I suppose it will be by selling it. We couldn't expect to make anything out of a blind man."

"Have patience," said Anne. "So it often happens in fairy stories—that great fortune comes from the last place to be expected. No harm is done—if no good. Remember we *must* be careful. You know how down they are in this town on anything that smells of magic. You remember how Agnes told us about their hauling her up before the courts for witchcraft. If we were questioned about where we got the shell and had to confess we got it from 'Shragga the Witch,' what then? We've got to think of her as well as ourselves."

"Yes, perhaps you're right," said Giles gloomily. "It would almost seem as though this town goes witchcraft mad every once in a while. Luke told me that even the old philosopher Johannes was not spared from their hunting and meddling. Just because he studies the science of alchemy, he had to be brought before the judges. Even harmless old Johannes."

"Johannes! That's an idea," cried Anne. "He at least would not give us away. And he would be interested too. He does not smell the Devil in everything new. Let's take the shell to him!"

The philosopher Johannes lived up in the hills behind the town. The children had visited him once before— by accident. They had been hunting blackberries and lost their way. They had blundered upon a tiny cabin. At first they had been frightened by the angry red face that popped out of the window. But presently, when the angry red face had heard their sad story, it invited them to come in while the road home could be explained to them. And finally they had gone away with no feeling of fear in their hearts for this man who lived alone in the hills.

Now without hesitation they made plans for a second visit to him. They would have to go home and get lunch first. The clock in the church tower was striking noon as they broke into a run.

Elsbeth the old cook quickly provided them with a light meal and they were on their way out again ten minutes after they arrived.

The trip was a long one, with a good deal of climbing. It took them two hours of hard travel before they stood before the door of the philosopher's little home. Giles knocked gently. The door was opened, just a crack, through which one eye looked forth suspiciously.

"May we come in and see you about something?" asked Anne. "We will not stay very long."

"Is anyone else with you?" asked the old man.

"No," said Anne. "We are alone."

The door was opened wide, the children passed in,

and it was closed again and locked—behind them.

The time before, when they had been inside the hut, it had been late in the evening and they had seen little or nothing of the philosopher's one-room home. But today, with a bright sun shining overhead, they were able to see the room clearly.

It was indeed a most unusual place. In some ways it reminded them of Agnes's little house; and yet it was very different. Everywhere there were bottles, crystals, queer glass balls, and pipes and things that are used in the study of chemistry. Everywhere, too, there were books: books on the table all mixed up with the bottles and chemicals; books in rows and piles upon the shelves; books on the floor in stacks; books on the little bed beneath the window.

And then there were smells. Anne's keen nose had never smelled so many gathered together in one small room before. Some were not unpleasant; some were very strong; and some were perfectly horrible. The worst one of all seemed to be coming from a small vessel set over a little charcoal fire in the corner. This, it would seem, was the chemistry work the philosopher was busy with when the children had knocked and interrupted him.

Giles inquired what the nature of this work was; and the philosopher, usually so grumpy and silent, seemed quite pleased to explain it. He at once started off into a long and learned explanation in which there was a lot about "salts of metals," "temperatures," "effects of mineral gases"—most of it far beyond the understanding of the children.

Anne watched the old man's eager face as he turned to explain the mysteries of chemistry to her young brother, and she guessed that it was many a long day since anyone had shown a friendly interest in his work.

"Aren't you ever lonely up here, sir?" she said when at last he paused.

"Lonely?" he said. "Er—no. Why should I be? No man is ever lonely if his work is what he lives for."

"But what do you hope to do with all this—"

It was Giles speaking. He broke off and, blushing a little with sudden shyness, waved his hand toward the cluttered benches that ran halfway around the walls of the room.

"With chemistry?" asked the old man. "Why, boy, we hope to do everything. Look here!"

The philosopher reached up to a shelf and lifted down a big glass jar filled with a curious amber-colored paste that might have been frozen honey.

"You see that," said he. "If I were to place that beneath a castle wall and set a flame to it, I could blow a hole in the ramparts big enough to march an army through, a score abreast. And then what use would be their archers and crossbowmen? The King, I reckon, would give me the price of half his realm for fifty barrels of that paste, in time of war. But"—he set the heavy jar back upon the shelf—"I do not work for the destruction of man. That stuff there I discovered by accident—and nearly lost my life when first it exploded."

"What are all these papers?" asked Anne, examining a pile of parchment sheets that lay on a side table.

"Oh, that's a book I'm writing," said Johannes.

"What's it about?" asked Anne, who, while she was very proud of what little reading she could do, was quite unable to make head or tail of this.

"It's a book on chemistry—a first book, an easy one," said the philosopher. "But it's in Latin. Can you read Latin?"

"No, I'm afraid not," said Anne in an airy tone which might mean that it was only by chance that she had not yet mastered that language. "But why do you write it in Latin?"

"Because," said Johannes, "Latin is the only language that all the world speaks—or, that is, that all the world reads—in books."

"You have written many books, sir?" asked Giles.

"Yes, quite a few," said the philosopher.

"We never see them in our schools. And yet they give us books on mathematics with figures and little jiggly things such as you have here," said Anne, turning over the pages.

The philosopher smiled.

"Well, you see," said he, "with this kind of work it is different. Chemistry—or alchemy, as many call it—is something that people still connect with witchcraft and deviltry. Your schools, you say? Yes, they will take in works on mathematics today; but only a few years ago they wouldn't do even that, mark you—at least nothing *new* in mathematics. Some day perhaps they'll let books on chemistry into the schools. But not now. No, we have to work like thieves behind closed doors and sealed windows, lest we be called wizards and witches for bringing forward anything new. . . . Anything new!" The philosopher suddenly threw his arms in the air, and his face got even redder than usual. "Anything new! That's what they're afraid of. They want to make the world stand still. Sometimes I believe they'd sooner see it go backward than forward. . . . But you said you wanted to talk to me of something, eh?"

"Oh, yes," said Giles, suddenly brought back to the real reason of their visit. "We have here a shell. It does unusual things. We thought that you, a man of science, would be interested in it—though we have an end of our own to serve in bringing it to you."

Slowly Giles brought the twisted green shell out of his pocket and laid it on the bench among the bottles and jars.

"Usually, sir," said he, "as of course you know, one only hears the roaring of the sea in an empty shell if he holds it to his ear."

"Yes, yes," said the philosopher. "I remember doing it myself as a child. Go on."

"But this shell does more than that," said Giles. "It tells you what anyone is saying about you anywhere in the world."

"What!" cried the philosopher. "Poof! Poof! Do you take me for a ninny, boy?"

"It is true, sir," said Giles. "Please believe us. This shell when carried in your pocket gives warning if anyone speaks of you."

"How?" asked Johannes.

"By growing warm," said Giles.

"But this is ridiculous," cried the philosopher. "It cannot be done."

"Sir," said Giles, "have you not in your chemistry here made wonders happen? Your paste that can blow a hole through a castle wall just with the touch of a spark. How is that done?"

"Tut-tut!" grunted the philosopher. "But all that I can explain. I can show you in figures and formulae, in diagrams and diameters, just how the paste works. But this! This is unexplainable."

"But, sir," Anne put in, "can we explain how any shell gives out sounds—noises like the sea? Why?"

"Oh, that is quite simple," said the philosopher. "The peculiar shape of a shell inside gives you an echo of all the little noises in the air about you which the naked ear cannot catch. The general roar sounds somewhat like the roar of the sea—which is also made of many small noises mixed together."

"Very well, then," said Anne, "why should not this shell have extra funny insides and carry the echo of voices better than anything else?"

"Humph!" grunted Johannes. "That's an interesting notion—very interesting. You talk much older than you look, young lady. I don't say I believe it, but it *is* an interesting thought. . . . Well, what is it you would have me do?"

"We want you to keep it, sir," said Anne suddenly, taking up the shell and pushing it into the philosopher's hands. "Just keep it—in your pocket always. We will come back later, by your leave, and see what luck you may have had with it."

Suddenly the pot on the fire boiled over, making a great sputtering in the coals. The philosopher leapt to attend it.

"Yes," said he: "Come back when you wish, children, I'm busy now. But you at least I shall always be glad to see—whether your crazy shell works or no. Knock two and two—*tap-tap, tap-tap*—so! Then I shall know it is you."

CHAPTER NINE

CHEMISTRY AND MAGIC

T*ap-tap!* . . . *Tap-tap!*

It was the children knocking on the cabin door next morning. They were not kept waiting long. Almost before the fourth tap had struck it, the door flew open, as if by magic. There stood the philosopher, a terrible frown upon his very red face. In his right hand, thrust out to them, he held the shell.

"Here it is," he said. "Take it and never let me see it again!"

There was a bang of the door slamming to. And the youngsters again stood alone outside. Speechless with surprise, they stared at one another across the shell that lay, where the philosopher had thrust it, in Giles's hand.

Then, dreadfully disappointed, they turned away from the cabin. After such a welcome there was nothing else to do but leave. They had not walked more than fifty paces, however, before they heard a voice call them.

Turning about, they saw the figure of Johannes standing on his threshold again.

"Forgive me, children," said he when they had returned to him. "Forgive me if I allowed my temper to get the better of me. I cannot have you go away like this. Hospitality, good manners—well, maybe I've forgotten all about them, living alone so long. Come in again and let me talk further with you."

Neither Giles nor his sister had ever before been spoken to in such a manner by any grown-up person, much less by a philosopher, a learned professor of mathematics, chemistry, and heaven knows what other sciences.

"It's my own fault—entirely my own fault!" Johannes kept muttering as he led the youngsters back into the cabin and closed the door. "I was tempted. Yes . . . Like any fool, I was tempted. Bah! My own fault!"

And he stirred the fire so roughly that sparks and coals flew everywhere.

"But, sir," said Anne gently, "how do you mean—your own fault? What has happened? What harm's been done?"

Almost savagely the philosopher turned from the fire and faced her, the poker in his hand. He looked for a moment like some little red demon about to spring upon an enemy.

"What harm?" he yelped. "You've ruined my peace—you and your shell. . . . There, there! You didn't mean to, I know. 'Twas I should have known better. But—

but—but—poof! But—but"—he spluttered almost like a rain-soaked candle—"how could I know the wretched thing would really work?"

"Well," said Anne very, very softly, "we told you it was peculiar, you know."

"Yes, yes," muttered the philosopher as he wiped his forehead of the sweat caused by the fire's heat and his own fussing. "You knew more than I—I with all my studying and labor. There's no science in it, no chemistry, no natural law, no sense whatever, and yet it works. If I were not a chemist, I would call it magic, I suppose. . . . Well, the greatest thinkers have warned us not to be proud of our little knowledge."

"Then you mean to say that something happened, sir," said Giles, coming forward eagerly. "You—you did hear voices?"

Again Johannes mopped his brow while with his poker he made another attack upon the fire, jabbing it viciously.

"Yes," he said at last. "I heard. I heard all the other scientists and alchemists and philosophers—all over the world—saying what they thought of my last book. And they didn't say one single decent thing. All bad. All bad. . . . Jealousy, that's what it is. At first I wouldn't listen and I laid the shell down upon a stool and went on with my work. Because, after all, what do I care what the silly dummies say? I know when I am right, don't I? Then unthinkingly I sat down upon the stool and the shell was hot and burned me—or I thought it had. And I knew that someone else was talking about me. I wondered if perhaps this time it might be something good, of scientific value, you know. So I took it up."

A third time the philosopher wiped the perspiration from his excited ruddy face.

"I hadn't meant to listen long," he continued, waving the poker desperately in the air. "And I wouldn't have done, only I heard old Hieronimus, the astronomer of Arles, talking about my theory of atmosphere and light. He is no fool, is Hieronimus of Arles—usually. And so I was tempted and listened on and on. I couldn't understand or explain how it was being done. But I wondered if some day scientists would come to look on this as an everyday usual thing—a voice speaking across hundreds of leagues from one man to another, with nothing connecting them but the common air between. Well, there they were: Hieronimus discussing my work with two charlatan quacks who clearly considered themselves learned doctors of high degree. This theory of air and light, mark you, I had spent years of work on and had set it forth fully in my last book. I *know* I am right. I can prove it. It wouldn't have been so bad if I could have talked back to them through the shell. But there I had to sit, hearing them chatter and twaddle on, getting further and further from the real truth all the time. Again and again I laid the shell aside and tried to work. But all the time I found I was arguing with them in my mind and mixing my chemicals and figures into a hopeless jumble. And I kept going back to listen for some more—like a half-wit. The result is, I haven't done a stroke of decent work since you left. You're just in time to save me from going completely crazy. Take it away now. Ah, what a relief it'll be to have it out of reach! Take it, quick, before the wretched thing gets hot again. I can't trust myself. I should have known better. So should Hieronimus. Get out, my dears. Good-bye!"

So great was the philosopher's haste to be rid of them that Giles and Anne found themselves bundled like potatoes out upon the turf before the door.

On the way home they consoled themselves by gathering the blackberries that now grew, plentiful and ripe, on the heath that covered the hills. They had had more than enough of the Whispering Shell for the present and did not speak of it again till they reached the town.

Passing through the marketplace, they were hailed by Luke the Lame Boy.

"What's the matter?" he cried. "Such glum faces—and all covered in blackberry juice! Why so sad?"

Then Anne, remembering Agnes's great trust in this lad, told him how they had a shell which let you hear what people were saying about you. And Giles broke in to explain how they had tried it on two people and neither of them wanted to keep it. And Anne told Giles not to interrupt and went on with what she had to say.

"You see, Luke, one of these people didn't have anyone talking about him; and the other had folks talking about him no end, but the things they said upset him and kept him from doing his work."

"Look, Luke," said Giles. "Here is the shell. Isn't it a beauty?"

The lame boy looked down at the green thing shining and flashing in Giles's hand. Then he turned away with a shrug.

"Well, for my part, neither would I want it," said he.

"Why?" asked Anne.

"Because I know already what people say about me."

Suddenly Giles felt his sister nudge him—apparently to keep him from asking any further questions. Awkwardly they bade the lame boy farewell and proceeded on their way. Anne glanced back over her shoulder to make sure they were beyond Luke's hearing before she spoke again.

"I don't know how I could have been so thoughtless," said she when they had reached the far side of the marketplace. "Of course the poor boy knows already what people say of him."

"Yes," sighed Giles, nodding seriously. " 'Ugly little imp! Misshapen little brat!'—and so on. Poor Luke! They are a heartless lot, the children of this town. I'd like to punch their heads when I hear them teasing him. Well, it doesn't seem that we have got any further with our shell, Anne. It's not so wonderful. Maybe, after all, it doesn't matter what people say about one?"

"I wish we could see Agnes again," said Anne. "Perhaps she would tell us more about it."

"I don't believe she would," said Giles. "People in fairy stories never tell you much. They just say, for instance, 'Take this ring, put it on your father's finger, and he'll turn into a black swan.' They never tell you who's going to feed him or where you're going to get a lake for him to swim in. You can just take your choice: your father or a black swan. No, people who deal in magic don't talk much."

"But this isn't magic," said Anne. "At least," she added thoughtfully, "I don't think it is. In any case, let us seek out Agnes. It would be fun to meet her again even if she won't say any more about the shell."

"All right," said Giles. "But for the present we must get home. It's late."

CHAPTER TEN

THE MAN WHO KNEW EVERYONE

That night the children found that a very important personage was to be a supper guest at their house. It was no other than Master Piers Belmont, Chamberlain to the Duke. Often enough had Giles and his sister gazed up at the great castle on the hill in the center of the town. The Duke's home! Great gray towers surrounded by lesser buildings, with all manner of different roofs, a chapel of its own, stables, smithies, and servants' houses, it was like a town in itself—a town within a town. It was the finest castle, folks said, in all that country—except perhaps for the King's, and he lived in a city a long way off.

But indeed to the townsfolk the Duke seemed like a king himself. He had an army of his own and officers of the household. And all the notices posted in the town, all the announcements cried aloud by the Town Crier, ended, "By order of the Duke." It had even been hinted that the King was himself a little afraid of this great man who, while he was His Majesty's subject and obeyed his commands, was also His Majesty's cousin. But that was only gossip. Certain it was, however, that the Duke, being the most powerful of all the nobles in the land, had often greatly helped the young King's father in his wars.

And now that a member of the ducal household was guest in *their* home, Giles and Anne were very excited. For hours they lay awake at their old game of listening to the clatter of knives and forks and the bits of talk that floated up to the attic. Next day they pestered their mother to tell them all that had been said.

Well, it seemed their father had persuaded the great Chamberlain to come and talk over his business affairs with him. He was the Duke's right-hand man in all matters of money and law. And he proved himself a learned gentleman and very wise.

"I never heard anything like him," said their mother. "He's been everywhere. He knows everyone."

"Was he able to help Father out of his money troubles?" asked Giles.

"Alas! No," said their mother, turning away sadly. "He could give us no advice that was helpful. Goodness! If a change of some sort doesn't happen soon, I don't know what is to become of us."

The children now set out on a hunt for Agnes the Applewoman. One of the first persons they called on to question was Luke the Lame Boy. He lived in part of an old tumbledown stable which a horse dealer let him use for his own. He often got odd jobs about the yard from the people who came to trade there, holding horses, carrying messages, and whatnot. This home of his was at least dry and comfortably lined with straw, even if it had been made for horses to live in. Indeed, Anne and Giles sometimes envied Luke his peculiar shelter, in the way young folk often do, thinking every place but their own home the finest in the world. Luke knew all the gossip of the town; and many a pleasant hour the children had spent sitting on his straw bed with him, chatting of this and that.

But today the lame boy could not help them in their quest.

"I have not seen the Applewoman in many weeks," said he. "I wish I had. My leg is troubling me again."

"What, your—your twisted one?" asked Anne with wide-staring motherly eyes.

"Oh, no," laughed Luke. "That one never was much good. It is this, my left one, that has failed me now. You see, using it so much, with only the crutch to take the place of the other one, sometimes gets it so tired, I am unable to walk. Agnes has always been able to put it right for me. She hopes some day to cure both. How long have you been seeking her?"

"Oh, not long," said Giles. "We only set out today."

"Well, I am almost certain she is not in the town," said Luke. "If she were, I would have heard. Why don't you look for her in the fields—in the country beyond the walls. She spends much time there hunting for the plants and roots from which she makes her medicines. If you find her, bring me word."

Thanking Luke, the children set off again.

The day had begun with the fairest of weather and they thoroughly enjoyed the sunny fields and cool lanes and all the glory of summer in the country.

But they saw nothing of Agnes.

Finally, pretty weary, they sat down to rest and eat their sandwiches. Their talk turned upon Piers Belmont, the Duke's Chamberlain.

"I'm not sure I think so much of him, after all," said Giles. "If a man with his knowledge of business, looking after all the Duke's money matters, cannot find a way to put Father's worries to rest, well, he can't be so great. That's what I say."

"Oh, but you can't tell, Giles," said his sister. "Father's troubles may be particularly hard to set straight. Master Belmont *must* be a great man. You remember what Mother said about him?"

"No," muttered Giles. "What was it?"

"She said, 'He's been everywhere. *He knows everyone.*'"

Anne folded her hands and with a sigh gazed up at some small gray clouds crossing the sky.

"I find nothing marvelous in that," said Giles.

"Oh, good gracious!" cried Anne impatiently. "Just think of it—*to know everyone!* Fancy traveling to a foreign country and going up to the King and saying, 'Well, here I am'!"

"Humph!" her brother muttered. "And I can imagine it's being a great nuisance, too, to know everyone. For, mark you, that means also to be known by everyone; having everyone poke his nose in your business; never to be able to go anywhere without someone saying he saw you do this or he saw you do that."

"Oh, but just think," said Anne, "every time you went into a church, or down the street, having *all* the heads turn and say, 'There goes Anne.' . . . I wonder how one goes about getting to know everyone. How many people do you know, Giles?"

"Oh, six or seven," said Giles. "That is, not counting Mother and Father and Uncle Remigius. I suppose family doesn't count. After all, you *have* to know your family— My goodness! Is that rain falling?"

"That's what it is," said Anne.

While the children had been talking, the heavens had become quickly overcast with heavy black clouds; and now great big single drops were splashing all about them with a promise of a regular downpour soon to come.

"Quick!" said Anne. "Let's run for that house down the road there. We can take shelter in the stable or something. We'll be drenched if we're caught in the open in a rain like this."

So off they ran. And the rain seemed to run behind them, growing and growing. Presently, when they reached the house, the shower had become so heavy that they did not hesitate or bother about whose place

it was. They ran straight up to the door and leapt
through it into the hall.

They were so breathless from running that it was a
moment or two before they began to look around them.
In the doorway through which they had come, the door
hung on one hinge, half leaning against the wall. The
walls were bare and had their plaster broken in many
places. The floor, too, had holes in it and was littered
with dust and dirt. It was a deserted house.

"Giles," whispered Anne, "do you know where
we've come to?"

Her brother nodded his head.

"Yes," he said slowly. "It's the Haunted Inn."

For another moment they were silent again while
both, with some fear and hesitation, gazed backward
into the shadows at the end of the hall. The rain outside
poured down into the yard and road with a steady hissing noise.

This house was one the children had often wished to
visit, but had never quite had the courage to. It was a
hostelry known in days gone by as the Golden Mitre. In
those times it had been famous for its wines and cooking
and for the good comfort travelers enjoyed there. But
for years now it had lain empty and abandoned. No one
knew why, but many said the place was haunted. Today
Giles and Anne had blundered into it unknowingly, in
their helter-skelter hurry to get shelter from the rain.

"Let's go, Giles," said Anne, clutching his hand and
turning again to the door. But the curtain of falling water

that barred the way out was almost as terrible as the house itself.

"Well," laughed Giles, "we can't very well leave now anyhow. Here we are, both of us, after all our daring each other to come in."

And then suddenly, as is the way with summer storms, the rain stopped and the sun came out. The shadows at the end of the hall grew less black as the new light shone dimly down through dirty windows above. Anne, who had been staying right at the edge of the doorway, stepped out at once and called to her brother. But Giles shook his head.

"No, wait a minute, Anne," said he. "Now we are in the Haunted Inn, let's look around a little. After all, there's nothing to be afraid of that I can see."

"I'm not afraid of what we can see," said Anne. "It's what we *can't* see that I'm afraid of. How about the ghosts, Giles?"

Her brother had now walked into one of the big rooms off the passage. It seemed to have been a dining hall in its day. A long broken table stood in the middle of the room and there was an enormous fireplace in the center of one wall.

"Ghosts?" said Giles as he strode across the floor. "What rubbish, Anne! I don't believe anyone ever really saw a ghost. And even if there were some here, what harm would they want to do us? Ghosts indeed! Poof! Oh, my gracious! What was that?"

A curious scratching sound had suddenly come from behind a cupboard door.

"Giles, something tells me we should be going," said Anne.

"No, now, just a minute," said her brother. "We've been brave enough to get in here, even if we did come by accident. And we've been brave enough to stay here for a while. Now the question is: Are we brave enough to open that cupboard door?"

"Well, you can soon settle that," said Anne. "Go over and open it."

"Why shouldn't *you* open it?" asked Giles.

"I don't choose to," said his sister. "I would sooner go outside and enjoy the air."

"All right, then, I'll open it," said Giles, putting on a very terrible and warlike face.

He went nearer to the cupboard while Anne looked on with wide-open eyes at her brother's daring. The noise had come from a closet door beside the fireplace. As Giles drew nearer, the scratching sound broke out again, but louder and stranger. He hesitated. Then he took hold of the handle. He wondered whether it would be wiser to open it just a crack and peep in or to pull it open suddenly and wide. He made up his mind that the last would be the best. He gave a tremendous tug.

The handle came off in his hand and he sat down on the floor with a big bang.

CHAPTER ELEVEN

AT THE HAUNTED INN

"Look!" said Anne. "The door is locked with a key. That's why the old handle broke off. You'll have to turn the key to open the door."

"Well, if the key's the right one, I'll open it this time and no mistake," said Giles. And without further ado he went up to the cupboard, turned the key, and pulled the door wide open.

And a big black cat walked silently out into the room.

"So much for your fears, Anne," laughed the boy. "We might have known that ghosts never scratch. First we were afraid to come into the house, and then we were afraid to open the cupboard. That's the way with most fears: They are always fears about what you don't know. Now, let's go all over the house and explore it from top to bottom. Then when we go back to the town, we can tell the people we have made a good job of the Haunted Inn."

"Giles," said Anne, "that cat there—doesn't he look like one of the cats that Agnes had?"

The big black animal seemed quite friendly, and after brushing himself against the children's legs, he walked slowly from the room.

"Oh, I don't know," said Giles. "All black cats are alike to me. Let's take a look around upstairs. Wait. Maybe I'd better close the cupboard again first."

As he went to fasten the door, Giles noticed an old tinderbox and two stumps of candles on a shelf within.

Then the children went upstairs.

"Be careful of the holes in the steps and the landings," said Giles, who was walking ahead. "Many of the boards are rotten. Tread lightly first before you trust your whole weight."

The rooms upstairs they found pretty much like those below, only worse. There was more plaster fallen from the walls, and the holes in the roof had let the rain spoil the ceilings in many places. More dust, more cobwebs, and more broken windows. Here, too, there was very little furniture. In the largest room, the one over the dining hall, there was another fireplace and an old broken-down four-poster bed, leaning awry with only two feet to stand on.

"Now let's go down into the cellar," said Giles.

"Do you think that is necessary?" asked Anne.

"Quite," said her brother, "if we are going to explore the place properly. Come along."

They found nothing very unusual in the cellar: shadows, a musty smell, barrels, more broken furniture, paintpots, and an old lantern, which they brought upstairs with them.

"Well," said Giles, puffing out his chest, "the deed is done. It wasn't so bad, was it? I wonder if there are any more haunted houses left in these parts. I am feeling pretty brave now—indeed, this is one of my bravest days. How do you feel, Anne?"

"I'm doing nicely, thank you," said his sister. "But one haunted house a day for me will be enough. I was just thinking, Giles, as we were coming up those cellar steps, the stone all worn into hollows by all the feet that must have trudged up and down them for hundreds of years—"

"Well, what about it?" asked Giles. "This was an inn, you know, where I suppose thousands of guests came a year. And all the food and wine for those people was brought up from the cellar. No wonder the steps are worn."

"Yes, that's just it," Anne went on. "I had been thinking again of what Mother said, about Piers Belmont knowing everyone. I suppose an innkeeper must have come to know an enormous lot of people in his lifetime. That would be as good a way as any to get to know everybody, being an innkeeper, wouldn't it? Oh, here's another closet! I wonder what's in this one."

They were now standing in what was clearly the

kitchen, since it had large ovens next to its fireplace and nails and hooks for hanging pots and pans. Anne opened the closet. At first she thought it was empty, but by standing on tiptoe she was able to see onto the higher shelves; and there she found two pieces of linen. On spreading them out she saw they were aprons.

"Oh, Giles!" she cried. "Let's put them on."

"What on earth for?" he asked.

"Why, then we can play at being innkeepers."

At first Giles was not very keen about the idea; but after Anne had persuaded him a little, he thought it might not be such a bad game and he tied his apron around his waist. In a flash they became Master Giles and Mistress Anne, the host and hostess of the Golden Mitre. As busy as monkeys they were, running up and down stairs; making make-believe beds; skipping in and out of the kitchen to serve make-believe meals; calling to Joe, their make-believe houseboy, to "fetch in those trunks and hurry about it, sirrah!"

Such a good time did they have, attending to the wants of a never-ending procession of travelers coming to and going from the inn, that they hardly stopped playing even when the rain came on again. However, when the water began driving into the passage through the front entrance, Master Giles called out of the window to his servant Joe to come in and fasten up the front door—"and be quick about it, sirrah!" But the hardworking Joe took so long about it that the master of the inn came down and did it himself. And no easy matter it was, with a door that had only one hinge left to hold it against the screaming wind. But he got an old broom handle to prop it, or strut it, at one corner, and it kept the storm out.

Then Anne spoke of how dark it had grown, and Giles fetched one of the candle ends he had seen in the cupboard and lit it with the tinderbox. This added something new to the game, and they went at it again, keener than ever, till at length, thoroughly tired, they sat down to take a rest.

By now the rain was really terrible, worse than it had ever been. The lightning flashed and flickered and the thunder made the old house rattle and shake from end to end.

"Wouldn't it be funny, Giles," said Anne, "if a real guest were to come along now."

"Funny?" said Giles. "What is the matter with you? This is a game, isn't it? Why would anyone come here?"

And then, as if in answer to his question, there came a *bang! bang! bang!* on the front door.

Both children sprang to their feet. For a while they stood staring at each other with their mouths open.

"Who-oo-oo can it be?" whispered Anne at last.

"How sh-sh-should I know?" stuttered Giles. "Why don't you open the door and see?"

"Why don't *you* open it?" asked his sister. "I don't think I'm strong enough to pull the prop away with the storm blowing so hard."

"Well, I opened the cupboard door," said Giles. "It's your turn now."

While they were arguing, the knocking broke out again even louder than before. Giles took the candle and went out into the passage and peered through the keyhole.

"There seem to be several of them out there," he whispered.

A third time the door shook to the thunderous knocking. And still poor Giles hesitated with his hand upon the broomstick which held the door to. And now the children thought they could hear the snorting and stamping of horses and the jingling of harness. But it was too dark to see very far beyond the door through a keyhole. Giles began to wonder what time it was. It should be only about four o'clock in the afternoon; but the darkness of the storm made it seem much later. Suddenly he felt the shell burning in his jacket. Who could it be that was speaking of him? He had started to reach into his pocket when a voice outside shouted: "Open! Open, I say! Would you have us drown out here?"

Without further delay Giles struck away the prop and the door flew inward before the wind and rain.

Standing on the threshold was a tall dark man. Rain dripped from the feather in his hat, from the hem of the big cloak that hung about his shoulders, from the tips of the embroidered gloves that covered his hands. He was evidently a nobleman. He hardly seemed to look at

Giles or Anne but strode past them while they peered into the darkness and the rain outside.

There they could now dimly see other figures moving about. Orders were being shouted. Then they thought they saw a coach—yes, a very grand and lovely coach—then two coal-black horses standing in the shafts. The flickering lightning glittered on their shiny, rain-soaked skins. A coachman got down from his seat and the horses were unharnessed and led away to the stables. And over and around the whole mystery, the rain splashed and streamed and hissed.

Presently the door of the coach opened and a woman got out carrying a small valise. In spite of the downpour she stood respectfully to one side, as though waiting for someone else still within.

And then there stepped from the coach the most beautiful and grandly dressed lady the children had ever seen. On the arm of the other woman (who was clearly her maid), she walked swiftly toward the door of the inn. But on the way two of the men came up and spoke to her, and Anne noticed that they addressed her as "Your Ladyship" or "my lady."

Inside the passageway she shook the water from the collar of her cape and spoke to Giles.

"I am indeed glad to reach the inn. What terrible weather! You are the host of the Golden Mitre?"

Giles looked blankly at his sister's apron and then at his own. The grand lady did not wait for his answer but turned to Anne.

"And you will be the hostess, of course. This is my maid, Margaret. Please lead us to my room. I am tired from the journey and would rest before supper."

Giles looked at Anne and whispered, "Supper!" And Anne looked back at her brother and choked, *"Supper!"*

"Please hasten," said the lady to Anne. "Lead the way. My lackeys will help you with the trunks," she called over her shoulder to Giles as she turned toward the stairs.

Poor Anne! She went forward with candle in her hand and her head in a daze. At every step upward she said to herself, "That awful room! With the broken-down bed! With the broken windows! With the dust on the floor! With the cracks in the plaster! What a dreadful place to put a lady to sleep! Oh, dear! Oh, dear! What shall I do?"

Well, she didn't do anything about it. She kept going straight on upstairs, as though she were bewitched and quite powerless to turn and tell the woman behind her what a dreadful mess she was taking her to.

And then, on nearing the landing, she thought she saw signs of a light, another light upstairs besides the one she was carrying. And when she reached the landing, she was sure. There *was* light, lots of it, shining from the big bedroom door. She ran forward to look in. Then she put her hand up to hold back a cry of surprise.

For the bedroom was all bright with many candles. The tumbledown bedstead was all set up with four feet and laid with lovely white linen, lace coverlet, and embroidered pillows. Gone were the dust and the cobwebs and the holes in the walls and the ceiling. The windows were washed and all the panes mended. And in the grate a warm fire was blazing up the chimney. Anne just gaped, unable to say anything.

"Truly, good hostess," said the gracious voice of the lady behind her, "I am both pleased and surprised that you've been able to provide for me so well. Yes, indeed, pleased and surprised I am."

"So am I, Your Ladyship," said Anne, finding her tongue at last.

Then she ran downstairs to look for Giles.

CHAPTER TWELVE

THE SUPPER AT THE GOLDEN MITRE

Below, Anne found more surprises. She rushed into the dining hall with her mouth full of the strange news from upstairs. But again she was struck silent. For that room was all lit up, too, with gay candelabra, and there was another jolly fire on the great hearth. The broken table stood all repaired and polished in the center of the room; and it was set with platters, knives and forks, bowls of fruit, goblets, and flagons of wine. Master Giles, the host of the Golden Mitre, was pottering to and fro at a great pace, fetching hams, turkeys, pasties, sausages, and whatnot from out of the kitchen, just as though it was a conjurer's hat. Two or three very richly dressed gentlemen were seated, drying themselves before the fire.

Giles had no time for his sister, and Anne had to run behind him out into the kitchen to get any word from him. There her chances proved not much better; for she found the coachman and four other servants seated at a wide table, gobbling bread and cheese and drinking ale from pewter mugs.

"But, Giles," she whispered as her brother bent down to pull still another joint out of the oven, "what is it? It's the same way upstairs. Everything bewitched, befuddled, bedizened. What is it? What's happening? Who are all these people? Where did all the food come from?"

"How should I know?" snapped the busy host. "I smelled it. Must have cooked itself. As for the people, why ask me? Some of those guests you were wishing for, I suppose. Maybe you were sitting on a wishing stone or something and didn't know it when you spoke. Anyway, here they all are and they have got to be fed. Take that bread knife there and chop that big loaf up into small hunks—only don't chop your silly fingers."

One thing that Anne spoke of later to her brother was that none of these strange people seemed to think the age and size of the host and hostess of the Golden Mitre at all unusual. It is true they spoke very little, either among themselves or to Giles and Anne. But that could very easily be because they were worn out from traveling. Tired men do not want to talk.

The supper was a great success. The servants, who had already eaten in the kitchen, helped Anne and Giles serve it. After it was all over, the great lady again praised and thanked her host and hostess for their service and excellent cooking.

Shortly after that she retired to her room for the night, and one by one the rest of the company also went to bed. The servants found themselves quarters over in the haylofts of the stables, while the gentlemen took the other bedrooms in the inn.

Then at last, for the first time in so long, the children were alone. And they sank into chairs on either side of the dining hall fireplace, wearily gaping at each other. Said Anne presently: "Well! Did you ever?"

And Giles answered: "No, I never did."

They were full of a thousand questions. But each knew the other could not answer them. So for a while they sat silent, lying back in the deep chairs and gazing at the glowing fire.

And there soon they must have fallen asleep. For the next thing they knew they were sitting on the floor, leaning against one another, terribly cold. There was no fire in the grate. The wind was blowing in through broken windowpanes. Dust lay on the broken table and cobwebs hung from the dirty walls.

It was morning.

"Giles! Giles!" said Anne at last in a trembling voice. "Tell me: Was I dreaming? Wasn't there a great feast laid on the table here last night?"

"Yes," said her brother, "and a company of grand people and—"

"And a very beautiful and highborn lady," Anne added, springing up, "who brought a maid with her and slept upstairs in a bed of fine linen, with lace. Why—!"

Without another word they both raced upstairs. At the open door of the big bedroom, they paused, staring. The grand lady and her maid were nowhere to be seen. The four-poster stood askew on its broken legs. The dust lay thick upon the floor. Everything was just as it had been when they first came to the inn and explored the rooms.

Giles grabbed his sister by the arm.

"The horses!" he cried. "Let's see if they're gone too."

A scamper down the stairs and out through the back door. A rush across the yard. And in a twinkling the big stable door was thrown open.

The only living thing to be seen was a large black cat, which came out to meet them, blinking in the new and sudden light.

Silently they went back into the house. They were barely inside when Giles felt the shell burning in his pocket again. He pulled it out and listened.

"It's Mother and Father," he said to Anne. "They're nearly frantic because we've been away all night. I can hear Mother crying her heart out, and Father stamping back and forth across the floor. Now they're talking again. Sh!"

For a moment Giles was silent. Then he burst out with: "Oh, my goodness, this is dreadful! Father thinks Agnes has kidnapped us. Shragga the Witch, as they call her—child stealing—and all that. Somebody saw us with her the other day when we went to the beach. Father is going to the Mayor to have her arrested. Quick! There's no time to lose. Let's get back home!"

Together they ran out of the dining hall. But at the door Anne caught her brother's sleeve and held him as she looked back for a last glimpse.

"It seems impossible, doesn't it?" she said slowly. "Here they all sat last night around the table, laden with good things to eat. And now this morning everything—everybody—gone! It can't have been a dream because we both saw it all. And two people couldn't have exactly the same dream."

"Yet—if somebody *made* them dream—I'm not so sure," said Giles.

"What do you mean, if somebody made them dream?" asked Anne.

"Well, if it's possible to *read* people's thoughts, maybe it's possible to *give* them thoughts. And Mother says that dreams are only the thoughts you think while sleeping. So perhaps someone might be able to make two people think the same thing while they were asleep. . . . Anyway, come. Let us be going. We've got to hurry."

Together they ran for the front door, knocked away the broom handle, and leapt out. Then before they could stop themselves, they had stumbled over a bent figure seated on the steps. They fell sprawling into the yard. The figure was Agnes the Applewoman. She rose and without a word walked into the inn.

"Agnes!" called Anne. "Agnes! We want to speak with you!"

The Applewoman paid no attention. They ran into the inn after her. But she was nowhere to be seen. They searched the rooms upstairs and the cellars below. Yet not a sign of Agnes could they find.

Suddenly Giles said: "Oh, my! That shell is burning again. Let's get home quick. We've got to stop Father from going to the Mayor."

And together they raced out of the house and down the road.

CHAPTER THIRTEEN

LUKE'S PLAN

They arrived just in time. Their father had his hat on and was about to go forth to the Town Hall to see the Mayor. Already there were several neighbors clustered about the gate, trying to comfort the parents over the loss of their children.

The return of Giles and Anne was greeted with great joy. Their mother, weeping for happiness, bore them off into the house. This they were glad of because they did not want to be questioned before the neighbors. Indoors, when both their parents and old Elsbeth the cook had done hugging them and thanking heaven for their safety, they had to explain their disappearance.

Giles was terrified he would be asked about Agnes and have to confess he had seen her since they were gone. So he started off right away to do most of the talking himself. He told how they had been overtaken by the terrible storm yesterday and had sought refuge in an old deserted house; how they had played there to pass the time, had got very tired, and finally had fallen asleep; and how they had not wakened till this morning, after daylight had come.

The only question they were asked was, what house was it they had stayed at. Giles did not want to answer this, but he had to. And when it became known in the town that he and Anne had explored the famous Haunted Inn and really and truly spent the night there, they became great heroes; and all the youngsters came around the next day to gaze at them and ask them about their adventure.

This same crowd of town children then went off to visit the Haunted Inn themselves. Which worried Giles quite a little. Since his return he had felt the shell burn again, and on listening to it he had heard Agnes talking to herself. "I do hope those little ones will keep a still tongue in their heads. If they get chattering about this inn too much, that will be the end of my peace here. I'll have to find another hiding place."

"Oh," said Anne when he had explained this to her, "then Agnes has been living there for some time. And that was why we couldn't find her. But what does she want a hiding place for?"

"I don't know," said Giles. "And, anyhow, that's not the important thing now. I've got to get back to the inn ahead of those children and warn Agnes. If they should see her there, they will tell about it in the town, and the gossips will begin to blame her for our disappearance, after all—for throwing a spell over us, or something.

There are too many people who are only looking for a chance to have her arrested for witchcraft. You stay here. If Father asks where I am, just say I've gone after the other children."

So, without further delay, he set out.

When he reached the inn, Giles was happy to find that Agnes had not been discovered. Lots of children were there, peering wide-eyed into the passages and rooms. But either the Applewoman had got wind of their coming and taken flight, or she knew some secret hiding place in the buildings that no one could find. Anyhow, there was no sign of her, and presently Giles managed to slip away from the crowd and made his way home alone.

Coming into the town, he noticed that there seemed to be a lot of excitement abroad. People were running toward the marketplace, chattering like magpies. Gentlemen on horseback were coming and going about the streets in all directions. Among them Giles recognized Master Piers Belmont, the Duke's Chamberlain.

On reaching the marketplace he found the fuss and commotion greater still. A large crowd of folk was gathered about the Town Crier, who was giving out a message to the people from the Duke. Giles elbowed his way in to listen.

The message was a long one and was all about a visit which the King was to pay the town. This was the first time that the new King had come here. He was going to stay at the castle with his cousin, the Duke, who wished the townsfolk to give him a worthy welcome and show their loyalty in a befitting manner. Then there was a whole lot more about a grand feast that was to be given in the King's honor the day of his coming, and of the special guards that were to be on duty certain hours of the day and night throughout the whole time His Majesty was here.

Giles hurried home to bring his sister the great news. But he found that it had got there ahead of him. His own home and the whole street in which he lived were in a great hubbub.

While the chatter was at its noisiest, the shell again grew hot in his pocket, and he listened to it.

It was two voices this time—Luke's and the Applewoman's. Without waiting to hear what words were passing between them, Giles grasped his sister by the hand and hurried out into the street.

"What is it, Giles?" she cried. "Not so fast! I can hardly keep up with you at such a gait."

"It was Agnes again," he called back over his shoulder. "Come on. Let's hurry. It was Agnes and Luke talking. She is bound to be at his stable—curing his leg most likely—because he can barely walk. If we're in time, we'll catch her. If we miss her, we'll maybe not get another such chance in goodness knows when."

But though they raced there as quickly as they could, they arrived too late. Luke told them that Agnes had come and gone.

"It's a big risk she took in coming here," said he as

the children sank down, disappointed, on the straw beside him. "Yes, a big risk—and for my sake. I think there is an order out for her arrest."

"Oh, is she charged with witchcraft again?" asked Giles.

"I'm not quite sure," said Luke. "I questioned her, but she wouldn't say. Everything had been all right for her for some weeks back, I know; and she had moved freely about the town. But she has mysterious ways of scenting danger. Myself, I fancy it may be this coming visit of the King's. The Duke is so fearful that something may happen to spoil the party for his royal guest. Well, who knows? I suppose once you've been accused of being a witch, you're never really safe. People may blame all sorts of accidents and misfortunes on you. So maybe Agnes feels it's wiser to keep out of sight just now. She's afraid of that stupid old Mayor—and he's afraid of her."

"Why?" asked Anne.

"Oh, I don't know," said Luke. "Most people are afraid of witches."

"But she isn't a witch," said Anne.

"No. Of course she isn't," growled the lame boy.

"Yet she can do magic, can't she?" asked the girl.

"I don't know," said Luke, frowning. "She certainly has done magic to my leg. I don't know what I'd do if I didn't have her to fix it for me when it lays me up. She has cured other people in this town too—those who trusted her. And I don't believe she ever did anyone any harm in her life. It's just that she is cleverer than other folk and wiser. She knows more. But I do wish she wouldn't keep those cats. People always think that witches have cats around them—that they are what is left of the poor souls they have enchanted. But Agnes won't give up her cats. She says that nothing anyone says will ever make her turn them out of doors."

"Well, I know I'd trust her," said Giles. "Why, she— Oh, my! There goes that old shell again. Hot as a chestnut!"

"Who is it this time?" cried his sister. "Get it out quick, Giles, and listen. I wonder, is it Agnes?"

She watched her brother's face as he held it to his ear.

"No," he said in a little while. "It's Mother and Father—and Mother crying again."

"What's the matter with her now?" asked Anne.

"Oh, it's that old money business again," said her brother. "Things are worse than ever, it seems. They're talking of selling the house to pay Father's debts. And they're wondering what is to become of us with no roof over our heads. Now they've stopped speaking of us and the shell's gone cold again."

"Oh, dear!" Anne said with a sigh as Giles ended. "I do wish we'd caught Agnes here today."

"Listen, Anne," said Giles. "Do you know whom I think we ought to take the shell to? Piers Belmont, the Duke's Chamberlain. You say he knows everyone. Well, a man with so many friends would be glad of such a thing. And he's rich. He could pay us well for it."

"Why not, better still, the Duke himself?" said Anne.

"Humph!" growled the lame boy. "And best of all, the King."

"The King?" gasped Giles in a hushed voice. "How could I dare—how could anyone like me reach the King?"

"It would not be much harder than reaching the Duke, maybe," Luke went on. "From what I hear, the King is by far the pleasanter gentleman of the two. He's well liked, this young King. Not much more than a boy himself. Nineteen years old. Set around by a lot of scheming relations and nobles, he should be glad of your shell— if it will work the way you say it will. It might help him in his business. The Lord knows he has his work cut out for him in governing this great land. Who in all the world has more folks talking of him, night and day? And for whom in all the world is it more important to know what's being said about him—and his affairs— than it is for a king?"

Giles was staring at the floor as Luke ended.

"The King!" he kept muttering, as though to himself. "The King! Well, *he* should be rich enough."

"Rich enough!" Luke said with a laugh. "Why, he could set your whole family up in comfort for life and pay your father's debts ten times over and never know that he had opened his purse."

They spent at least another hour with Luke—talking and working out plans. Giles feared that he would never be able to reach the King. While Luke stuck to it that it was the only thing to be done.

"But it's going to be no easy matter," said the lame boy. "And certain it is that you cannot trust the shell in other hands to be taken to the palace for you. For one thing, it is too precious. It is the only one of its kind, and if it be lost or stolen, your great chance to help your father's fortunes will be gone. And for another, should news of such an unusual thing as a whispering shell get about the court, you would be questioned—made to tell where you got it. And then poor Agnes would get into more trouble about witchcraft—most likely she'd be charged by the Mayor or the Duke with trying to cast spells over His Majesty himself. No. You, and you alone, have got to put that shell into the King's own hands."

"But why shouldn't they arrest me for witchcraft?" asked Giles.

"Oh, pooh, pooh!" said Anne. "Who ever heard of arresting a boy like you for witchcraft—with your freckles and snub nose? A fine witch!"

"My nose doesn't turn up nearly as much as yours does," said Giles. "Keep your remarks to yourself."

"She's right, Giles," said the lame boy. "You're safe on that score, I think. Your being so young is the best protection you could have. You stand a better chance of getting near the King than a grown person would. Your biggest danger lies in having your plans found out by others before you speak to His Majesty yourself. If you fail once, you will not likely get a chance a second time."

"But what if His Majesty himself accuses me of sorcery? What if he refuses to listen to me, to have anything to do with me?"

"You will have to take your chance of that," said Luke. "I don't believe he will, though. He has a name already for being just and fair-minded, and his reign only began a little while ago."

"It is a good thing the King is here now," Anne put in. "For there's surely no time to lose, with Father so hard pressed that he's about to sell the house over our heads."

"That's very true," said Luke. "All right, then, if you're willing, Giles, let us lay our plans."

"Couldn't he just go to the palace and say that he has a message for the King?" asked Anne. "After all, it is a kind of message, isn't it?"

"No," said Luke. "The King will be much too closely guarded for that. Your brother would be questioned by a dozen people and any message would have to be carried in by someone else. You see, the King has enemies, people who want to take his crown away from him and whatnot. So there will be the greatest care taken over who is allowed to come near him."

Then the lame boy told them just how he thought the business should be done. And in the end they both agreed with him and went home.

CHAPTER FOURTEEN

HIS MAJESTY COMES

It was a great day when the King entered the town. All the streets were gay with bunting and colored poles. Great arches had been set up with pictures painted on them. From almost every window hung garlands of flowers and silken scarves. And all the people were dressed in their best clothes.

The royal party, greeted in the marketplace by the Mayor and all the notables of the city, was made up of many persons, many horses, and many coaches. It was a big long procession—so long that when the head of it had reached the marketplace, the tail of it was still stretching away off into the country outside the town.

Anne, watching it come in, wondered how all those people and horses and baggage were going to find room within the Duke's castle; while Giles fell to dreaming over what it must be like to be a king. For he could not take his eyes off that young man on the beautiful white horse, who kept rising in his stirrups and with smiling face and waving hand answered the roar of welcome that came from the people. Giles had never known the town held so many men, women, and children. There seemed to be seas of faces wherever you looked. The streets were full of faces, the windows and the doors were crowded with faces—even the roofs of many houses were covered with people who had risked their necks to get places to see the King.

Giles, when he had heard the roar in the distance as the King's party had first come in sight, had felt a sudden sinking of the heart. What a mad plan it seemed, for a mere townsboy to hope to reach the ruler of the land, one so great and so important! But now, when he could see the King's face, his courage came back to him. He joined in the waving and the shouting of welcome. For the young King's face was not only very handsome, but it was a very honest face and kind—the sort of face you trusted from the first glimpse. Very different it was from the face of the Duke, his cousin, who rode beside him. That, too, was handsome but harder and prouder—and many, many years older.

For those on the crowded pavements, especially for shorter folk like Giles and Anne, it was almost impossible to tell what was going on. The noise and crush were most confusing. But presently they saw that the King and all the mounted gentlemen of his party had come to a standstill and that the Mayor was making a speech.

It was all about how glad everybody was to see His Majesty the King and how proud the town felt on this great day when he had come to pay it his first visit.

Presently, after the Mayor had ended and some more speeches had been made, the royal procession moved out of the marketplace and disappeared slowly through the gates of the castle. But it was not till quite a little later that the crowd began to break up. And even then Giles and Anne had hard work to make their way homeward through the press of slowly moving, tight-packed people.

The merrymaking and celebrations in the streets went on late into the night. But even without that noise Giles, for one, would have found it hard to sleep. For it had been agreed between him and Luke that tomorrow should be the day for him to try to see the King. He had not forgotten the lame boy's warning that if he failed in his first try, he would most likely never get another chance—and, quite possibly, find himself in prison instead. And nearly the whole night through Giles was going over in his mind just how he ought to do it, and thinking of the many slips he might make and the accidents that could happen.

But he did get some sleep toward the morning. And when he awoke, he found that the day was a bright and sunny one. Luke had promised to meet him not far from the palace gates. And as soon as he had swallowed some breakfast, he put the shell in his pocket and started forth. Anne followed just far enough behind to keep her brother in sight. She had a very worried look on her face and a wondrous new admiration for him in her heart.

When he reached the place where he was to meet Luke, he was disappointed to find no one there. But soon he heard a whistle and on looking about him saw the lame boy across the street in a deep doorway, making signs for him to come over and join him. This he did, and Luke drew him back into the shadows.

"See," said Luke, "we can get a good view of the castle gates from here without being seen."

"But how do we know the King will come out this way?" whispered Giles. "There are other gates to the castle."

"Yes, but this is the main one and will almost surely be used by the King," said Luke. "Now, pay attention to me: I did a little listening among the soldiers of the guard when they were talking in the taverns last night. It seems the King is going out hunting this morning. Most likely a party of gentlemen will be with him and some servants and huntsmen. You see those soldiers walking up and down there?"

"Yes," said Giles. "I'd hate to get a crack from one of those big ax-things they're carrying."

"Well, those men are only the sentries," Luke went on. "Now, just before the King appears, a whole lot more soldiers will come out from the castle yard. And they'll line up along the bridge over the moat. But they will leave the way clear for the King and his friends to pass through. They always do the same for the Duke. It is to keep the people from crowding up too close. Mustn't it be awful to be a king and have such a lot of fuss made every time you want to go out for a walk?"

"Yes, but how am I going to get near him," asked Giles, "when he's surrounded by soldiers?"

"That's just your chance," said Luke. "The people will crowd up behind the soldiers, trying to get a look at the King going by. And you, Giles, have got to be in the front row of those people, just behind the soldiers. Then, when the right moment comes, and the King— By the way, you will recognize him, won't you? He'll likely be dressed quite differently from yesterday— maybe riding a different-colored horse. But you'd know him anyway, wouldn't you?"

"I—I think so," said Giles. "I got a good look at his face when he was standing in the marketplace."

"Well, if you're not certain," said Luke, "we'll have to give it up for today. Because if you should stop the wrong man, goodness only knows what might happen. But I'll be there beside you to help make sure of him. Now, as soon as he comes right opposite you, you'll have to dive right through the soldiers, through their legs if need be. You're small, that's one thing. Then stand right in front of the King, so he'll have to stop. Hold up the shell and say you beg leave to speak with him."

"Oh, my!" muttered Giles. "It sounds awful scary. I'm glad I have you with me, Luke. You'll nudge me when you think everything is all right, won't you?"

"Yes, I'll be just at your elbow. . . . Listen! Do you hear those trumpets inside the walls? That means the soldiers are getting ready. The King will soon be coming out."

From their doorway the two boys now saw the townsfolk begin to gather at the gates. Every passerby stopped and added himself to the throng till soon there was quite a crowd waiting.

Luke decided this was a good time for both of them to come forth and mingle with the people so as not to be noticed. And Giles was astonished at the speed and ease with which the lame boy dug his way through the crowd, on one leg and a crutch, without being knocked down. It was clearly something at which he had had much practice.

But for the most part poor Giles paid close attention to the castle gates that hid all the glory of princes' lives from common view. And when at last the two enormous wooden doors began to swing slowly open, his heart was pattering very fast, his eyes were wide-staring, but about his mouth and jaw there was a firm and steady look.

Standing on the threshold of the castle yard, six lads could now be seen, brightly dressed in gay uniforms, with six shining trumpets held ready at their lips. They were very still, very silent. But all at once, when the doors had swung the whole way open, they blew a mighty blast of sound.

When the music had died away, things began to bustle. The trumpeters drew back to one side, and a soldier, clearly an officer of the guard, came forward and gave some orders to the sentries. These began herding the people back from the gateway, and soon a larger body of troops (about a hundred men, Giles guessed) marched out and formed up along the sides of the street.

"Good!" whispered Luke. "The King will be going out by the east. Let's move farther down, close to the bend, by the fountain. The people are fewer there—and the soldiers not so many. But we must not get too far away, or the horses will be trotting instead of walking. Oh, goodness! There he comes. Let's hurry."

Again with surprising speed the lame boy broke into a hobbling, hopping run, and in a couple of minutes the two had taken up a position on the line of march a hundred yards or so farther down the street. Here Luke became still more careful that they should not attract notice from anyone. And with Giles at his heels he sidled in through the crowd till the two of them had their noses almost touching the back of an enormous soldier.

This morning the people were not shouting as they had been yesterday. That had been a day of welcome. Now they were just very respectful and quiet. And no one would have guessed what they were waiting for if it had not been that all the men and boys took off their hats as a party of horsemen came trotting out from the castle gate.

Giles's heart sank as he saw the pace they moved at. It would be no easy matter for a boy of his size to stop a mounted man at the trot. But the party slowed down to a walk as soon as it had passed the bridge over the moat.

"Fine!" whispered Luke. "The King is riding right in front. That's he in gray, with the scarlet feather in his cap. Move a little to your right . . . a little more—so you're between the two soldiers. Steady! Don't press forward yet. Wait till I nudge you."

To poor Giles it seemed hours while the gray figure on the beautiful white horse walked down that hundred yards of cobbled road. A few paces behind came five or six noblemen—and behind them again, twenty or thirty servants or huntsmen. Everyone was mounted. As they came nearer, Giles, without stretching his neck too far forward between the soldiers, tried to see the faces of the horsemen behind the King. He somehow felt more afraid of them and the soldiers at his elbow than he did of the King himself. He looked for the proud dark face of the Duke. But it was not there. The King was going hunting today without the company of his cousin.

Then Giles heard a gentle whinny; and suddenly his wandering gaze found that the head of the white horse had come almost level with him. At that moment a bony hand pushed him softly in the back.

In a flash he had ducked under the soldier's arm and leapt out into the open roadway.

From then on things happened so fast that he could scarcely remember afterward the order or the nature of them. So anxious was he that the King should not pass that he grasped the royal bridle with his right hand while he held the shell up with his left. The horse reared in sudden fright and snatched its reins out of his fingers. A gasp of horror broke from the people. The big soldier jumped for the boy with his terrible halberd raised to strike. But somebody's crutch got tangled up in his legs and he came down with a clattering crash upon the cobbles, while his helmet rolled across the street. One of the noblemen spurred his horse forward to ride Giles down with drawn sword. In the wink of an eye the boy would have been killed. But the King, with his horse still rearing on two legs, struck the sword upward with his riding whip. Two more soldiers sprang out of the ranks with murder in their eyes and their lances lowered to run this daring urchin through.

"Stand away there!" roared the King. "Who gave you orders to leave the ranks? The boy has no weapon. He's not trying to kill me. What's the matter with you all? Be still—everyone!"

CHAPTER FIFTEEN

THE KING LISTENS TO THE SHELL

The royal command quieted the uproar in an instant. But Giles, now too scared and breathless to speak himself, felt the shell burn in his hand as the hundreds of onlookers put their heads together and whispered about him and his mad deed.

The King patted the neck of the beautiful white horse, which was still tossing its head and snorting nervously.

"There, there, Africa," he was saying, as though talking to a baby. "Everything's all right now. Settle down, my beauty, settle down."

In silence His Majesty straightened the cap on his head and threw away his broken riding whip. Instantly one of the noblemen moved forward and give him his.

"Listen, young man," said the King at length, looking at Giles with a slight frown. "You mustn't jump out suddenly in front of horses like that, you know. You wouldn't like it if you were a horse. You gave my Africa a fine fright. What do you want? What's that in your hand there?"

"Sh-sh-sh-shell, Your Majesty," the boy stuttered out at last.

"A shell!" said the King. "You risked your neck and scared us all like that for a shell!"

"I—I—I wanted to give it to you," said Giles.

"Well, that's very kind of you," said the King, a sort of half smile lurking around his mouth. "But what am I to do with it?"

At last Giles, encouraged by the King's manner, found his tongue. And in a moment he was talking away as though his life depended upon it.

"It's a whispering shell, Your Majesty. If you keep it in your pocket, it grows warm when anyone speaks of you—anyone anywhere in the world. And if you take it out and listen while it's hot, you'll hear what's being said."

"Boy," said the King, suddenly scowling, "if you're trying to make a fool of me, you'll find yourself in trouble."

"Oh, I'm not, Your Majesty, I'm not," cried Giles. "I beg of you, believe me. I've tried it myself and I know."

The King stared at him hard for a moment. Then he held out his gloved hand.

"Give it to me," he commanded.

At that Giles slipped the shell behind his back. And another hushed gasp of astonishment rose from the crowd.

"Your Majesty—forgive me—I can only do that if you'll promise me two things."

"Saints preserve us!" muttered someone among the bystanders. "He bargains with the King."

Again His Majesty gave the boy a long steady look, puzzled. But it ended in another half smile.

"Very good," he said. "What are your two conditions?"

"One is: I must have money. It's for my father, Your Majesty. He has lost all he has and is about to sell his home to pay his debts."

"Oh," said the King. "So you want to sell me the shell, eh? And what is the other?"

"The other is that I must have Your Majesty's promise that you will not ask me where I got the shell."

"Indeed! You're a good businessman even if you are small," said the King. "Very well, then, you have my promise. I'll pay your father's debts with two hundred crowns besides. And where the shell came from I will not ask. Now will you give it to me?"

"I thank Your Majesty," said Giles with a deep sigh and he held up the shell.

The King took it in his hand—then instantly dropped it. Giles caught it and gave it back to him.

"Do not be afraid of the heat, sir," he said. "You see, so many people are nearly always talking about Your Majesty that for you it would be warm almost all the time. The more people there are talking, the hotter it grows. But it never gets so it burns the skin."

The King examined it for a moment and then lifted it slowly to his ear.

"Oh!" he said at once. "There are so many, many voices. All talking at once. 'The King this and the King that.' But I can hardly make anything out plainly. It is all so confused and mixed up. Like a crowd chattering."

"Indeed, sir, that is what it really is: The crowd all about you here whispering and speaking of your escape from accident when I scared your horse. If you will command the people to be silent, you will likely hear more clearly. But you will find a better time to listen about midnight, when most folk are abed and only few are talking, even of the King."

His Majesty seemed now to be quite excited about his new possession and he gave orders to one of the noblemen to bid the crowd be strictly silent. And in the solemn hush that promptly followed, he held the shell again to his ear.

"It is still quite noisy and mixed up," Giles heard him mutter. "Oh, wait now . . . Yes . . . Now I get it . . . Single voices—quite clearly . . ."

Of all the people gathered about the royal party, Giles, standing with his shoulder against the muzzle of the white horse, had the best view of the King's face. For a long time the slim figure in gray with head bent down to listen was very still. Almost the only sound that could be heard was a gentle pawing on the cobbles—the beautiful Africa was impatient to go ahunting.

At the beginning the King's face had only showed eager smiling interest, almost like a boy trying a new toy to see if it would work. But as Giles watched, he saw many new expressions pass across it: first a sudden puzzled frown; then, more slowly, a look of horror that changed to anger; next a great sadness, a bereft, almost lonely disappointment; and at last a strange aging, a hardening, as though in a few moments this gay handsome youth had grown much, much older.

And Giles knew that the Whispering Shell had brought very serious and important news to the ruler of the land.

But when the King ceased to listen and raised his head, the crowd saw nothing in his face but proud and calm command. He paused a moment, as though thinking out a plan of action. Then he turned and called one of the noblemen to him out of the group behind.

"Godfrey," he said to the young man when he had gained his side, "how many have you in this party?"

Although the voices were kept very low, Giles caught every word that was said. The young man (who, Giles afterward learned, was generally known as Count Godfrey, Keeper of the Great Seal) looked backward over the line of horsemen before he answered the King.

"About fifty, all told, Your Majesty."

"How many are my men and how many are the Duke's?"

"They are all yours, Sire, except the six huntsmen, the Duke's Head Falconer, and the Captain of the Guard."

"Good!" said the King. "Send the Captain of the Guard back into the castle on some excuse. Let me see. Tell him to bring me a spare horse. Yes, that's it. Say I want Midnight, the black mare. Let one of my own grooms ride her. No hurry, you understand. If he overtakes us by midday, it will be time enough. Go now and get rid of him. I will await you here. And after you rejoin me, Godfrey, remember, if you love me, you will stick to my side like a shadow till this day's over."

The young man turned and trotted back along the line of standing horsemen. The King remained looking down for a moment at the shell in his hand.

"Magic?" he muttered. "I thought the days of magic had gone by. Magic or madness? Or a dream? Yet why not? They still would come to touch me for the King's evil. Well, there it is: It works. A shell—with a roar of voices in it, instead of the roaring of the sea."

Then suddenly he handed it back to Giles.

"But, Your Majesty," said the boy, "don't you want to keep it?"

"Yes, indeed I do," said the King. "But I want you to carry it for me. I am taking you with us, you see. Can you ride a horse?"

"Only if he walks, Your Majesty."

"Well, never mind. For the present you can ride with Count Godfrey. Get your arms tight around his waist and you won't fall off. He's a lightweight himself and his horse is stout. Later perhaps you can ride Midnight, my own black mare. You'll like her. She's very gentle. Not as fast as my Africa here. But fast enough, clever and surefooted— Ah, here comes Count Godfrey back. Now we can start."

CHAPTER SIXTEEN

MIDNIGHT THE BLACK MARE

In spite of the calmness shown by the King, Giles was sharp enough to guess that he was partly acting. He felt sure that big doings were afoot and that His Majesty did not want anyone for the present to know what they were.

The party got moving at once and it was barely clear of the narrow streets of the town before the pace changed to a trot, and then to a smart canter. Giles, with his arms around Godfrey's waist, was none too comfortable, but he felt quite safe. The Count was mindful of the King's request and kept his horse neck and neck with Africa the swift.

The straggling houses that lay outside the town began to disappear and soon even the lonely farm cottages could be seen no more. The landscape became, for the most part, rolling heath and moorland, with copses of trees here and there. After some miles the King left the roadway and led the party off across country. He seemed to be making for a large wood that lay along a high ridge. This, Giles thought, seemed like the beginning of a range of hills, for the ground kept rising up and up. He had never been so far outside the town before and he was beginning to look about him with the adventurous feeling of an explorer—in spite of the bumping and jogging of the horse.

Presently they reached the wood. They followed along the edge of it a little way and went in by a winding road which led, still upward, through thick-trunked beech trees and tall firs. Later they left even this woodland trail and, bringing their horses to a walk, struck right into the heart of the forest. Over furze and mountain brooks the way now had to be picked with nothing for guide but the sun and the slope of the land. The King did not give the order to halt until they had traveled in this fashion many miles. At last, suddenly, they came out into a small open glade.

It was a lovely spot: a circle of mossy turf surrounded by thickets of brambles and blackberries, with oak trees standing farther back—the sort of place that children would pick out for a secret playground. For while wonderful views of the country down below could be seen in many directions, the glade itself was well screened and almost impossible to see from the flat land farther down. Indeed, it would have been hard enough to find, even if a man set out to hunt for it, unless he stumbled on it by luck.

By this time everybody was glad of a chance to rest. But all waited for the King to dismount before getting down from their saddles. Giles felt pretty sore in several spots, but he was too excited over the great happenings he was taking part in to bother about a little thing like that. However, he had not guessed how big a part he had been playing; and more surprises were in store for him.

The King's manner appeared quite changed when at last he stood upon the ground and let the panting Africa wander free about the turf. The King seemed suddenly to have become businesslike and was in no mood to waste time. He at once ordered the chief huntsman to take his men and dogs and go in search of game. As soon as they were out of sight, he called to the remainder of the party (which was now made up of none but his own friends and retainers) and bade them gather about him in a close ring. And when he spoke, it was in a grave low voice that seemed to be trying to keep back anger, indignation, and maybe even tears.

"Gentlemen," he said, looking steadily into the faces of the noblemen nearest him, "I have been betrayed. And my own cousin, the Duke, is the traitor. He, and perhaps others of my family, have hatched a plot to hold me a prisoner in the castle we have left, to take my crown from me and set another in my place upon the throne."

A gasp of horror went up from all who heard. Whispered words of revenge and threats of violence broke out here and there. And a general rustle of movement swept through the whole crowd like a wind as it pressed still closer about the King.

"Luckily," he went on, "we have been given a chance to get a start on our enemies. They do not yet know that we have been informed of their treachery. But it will not be so for long, you may be sure. That is why I have sent the Duke's huntsmen off—in order that I may tell you of this and prepare ourselves for action. All of you, I know, I can rely upon. But I must make sure of these men in my cousin's service before we can go forward."

"But, Your Majesty," cried one of the nobles, "we can make short work of them. There are some thirty of us against half a dozen."

This speech was greeted by more threats of bloody vengeance. But the King held up his hand for silence.

"We want no violence or bloodshed that can be avoided. I will speak with them when they return and see how they take it. After all, they are but retainers, and we cannot blame them for the black evil in their master's heart— Ah! I hear them. When they come near, do you move around them in a circle to be ready. But remember, none is to be harmed unless he tries to escape and carry word to the Duke."

Silently then the noblemen and the King's retainers spread out around the glade in a ring. And when the huntsmen entered it, Giles saw that they had with them the King's black mare Midnight. She was ridden by a groom wearing His Majesty's livery. This man had fallen in with the huntsmen while he was searching for the King's party. Giles thought he had never in his life seen such a wonderful horse—not excepting even Africa—so graceful, proud, and dainty she looked, prancing across the glade toward the King with the hunting dogs about her heels. He felt that if *he* were a king and could have anything in the world for the asking, the first thing he would demand would be a horse like Midnight the black mare.

The Duke's Head Falconer, with his men following close behind, came up to His Majesty and started to tell him about some deer tracks they had found farther down the hill. But he hesitated and then stopped when he noticed that the King's own people were closing in upon him with a strange hard look in their eyes and their hands upon their sword hilts. Then very quickly the King told him what he had discovered, and from the surprise on the falconer's honest face, everyone felt sure that he and his men had known nothing of the plot.

"But you see," the King ended, "how I cannot possibly let you go back to the castle. It is not that I fear you would wish to take part in the Duke's evil plans against me; but when it is discovered that I have not returned tonight, my cousin will get suspicious that I have escaped and you will be questioned. Therefore I must take you with me."

The Head Falconer took off his hat and knelt on one knee before the King. His men behind him did the same.

"Sire," said he, "it is true that we are the Duke's men and would do our best always in his service. But we owe allegiance first to you as King of all the land. You can trust our loyalty. Yet if we come with you, what shall happen to our families should the Duke wish to take vengeance against them for our desertion?"

"You are not the only ones with that to fear," said the King. "Will not I myself have to leave behind many of my followers—yes, and relations, too, the Princess Sophronia my aunt, the young Countess Barbara, and many other ladies and gentlemen of my court who came upon this visit with me? Our best hope lies in keeping the Duke ignorant as long as may be of what has become of me and of what I mean to do. He can hardly suspect till tomorrow. And when he does, his first thought will be for his own safety, rather than taking vengeance on those we could not take with us. If my plans go well, he will, by tomorrow night, be no longer a duke. He will rather be a prisoner in my hands or a fugitive, very far from here, flying for his life. Once we are beyond the limits of his dukedom, I will raise an army big enough to deal with him and all his troops. And we will be back tomorrow at his castle gates to see to it that never again shall he have a chance to betray the guests that trusted him."

Turning from the huntsmen, the King now talked

quickly with Count Godfrey. There was much to be arranged and decided on. The whole of this big party had to get across the borders of the Duke's lands without being seen and by the shortest way. This meant finding guides who knew the trails used only by shepherds and such and those mountain paths along which no one would be likely to be met. Strict orders were given that if the party did meet any wayfarers, they were to be captured and taken along with it.

As it turned out, the Head Falconer and his men were the best guides in the whole country for such travel. Then fast messengers had to be sent ahead to the nearest points beyond the borders where the King's troops were stationed. These messengers were to carry signed letters from His Majesty ordering the commanders to put their men under arms at once and gather at a meeting place in readiness for the march against the Duke. Scouts had to be sent out ahead along the line of the King's flight to keep watch for any soldiers that the Duke might have encamped in unsuspected places. And there were a lot of other arrangements that had to be attended to besides.

All these matters the King handed over to Count Godfrey. The Keeper of the Great Seal wasted no time but went swiftly through the crowd gathered in the glade and gave short, sharp orders here and there. And soon there was a big bustle and a stirring, with men mounting their horses quickly and slipping away quietly among the trees. Even the dogs, trained in keeping silence and tracking down scents, did their part. In twos and threes they went off with the huntsmen to scent out the presence of dangerous men and protect their King in his flight.

While these things were being done, the King drew Giles aside and bade him sit down with him upon a mossy bank in a corner of the clearing. He looked at him a moment or two without speaking.

"Boy," he said at length, "the time will likely come some day when you're an old man and have grandchildren of your own, little youngsters about your own age now. And then you'll be able to sit back in your big chair by the fire and tell them a wonderful story, the story of how you saved the King's life. For you surely saved mine this day, boy—you and your Whispering Shell. It was a narrow escape. I heard that treacherous cousin of mine, as plain as though he were standing next to me, arranging with his brother and two other villains how they would put a drug in my drink and get me down into the dungeon before I woke up again. And then— Oh, but Heavens! Let's not talk of that now. It makes me feel too sick at heart. In his own house, at his own table, as a guest, I was to be caught—trapped!"

As the King stopped talking, Midnight the black mare (who seemed to follow her master about rather like a pet dog) came up and pushed her nose against his bent head.

"But surely, Your Majesty," said Giles, "even if the Duke had thrown you into prison, he wouldn't have killed you, would he?"

The King looked up and tapped Giles upon the knee with his finger.

"Boy," he said, "once prison doors have closed upon kings whose crowns are wanted by someone else, they are very seldom ever seen again—alive. No. He wouldn't have done it with his own hands, I suppose. But I would have disappeared just the same. You saved me. And I will not forget— Tell me: Is there anything you'd like—I mean besides the money for your father— anything you'd like for yourself, as a present?"

Giles's eyes suddenly sparkled. His chest heaved with a breathless sigh.

"Oh, Your Majesty, could I—could I have Midnight— for my own?"

The King suddenly shook off his serious mood and laughed outright. He rose to his feet and lifted Giles into the mare's saddle.

"I would sooner you had asked me for half my kingdom and a princess, the way they do in the fairy tales," said he. "But if Midnight's what you want, you shall have her. Be good to her. She's yours, boy—your very own."

CHAPTER SEVENTEEN

THE FLIGHT TO THE CAPITAL

From this point on it seemed to Giles that things happened faster still. It was all very confusing and it was made more so by his soon finding that he was very weary and almost falling alseep from time to time.

The journey to the border was a long one and the greater part of it was done under cover of darkness. For a boy who was not used to long riding, such a trip was a hardship. Before night came on, the King noticed Giles's weariness and had him shifted from the black mare to one of the horses ridden by a retainer. Here he was strapped on behind the other rider so that if he should be overcome by sleep he would not fall and hurt himself.

In spite of the difficult going, they made few halts for rest. At one of these the shell was used again. Giles was unfastened and lifted to the ground, and he got it out of his pocket and gave it to the King. It was late at night now and there were not many people out of bed. The King wished to learn if the Duke had sent any soldiers in pursuit yet. But though he could hear officers giving orders about searching for him, no towns or places were mentioned, so of course he could not tell how near these searching parties were. He even heard his cousin speaking of him, but it was mostly about plans for tomorrow. And the King felt sure that even if his staying so long away had caused some surprise and worry, no one at the castle suspected as yet that he was really trying to escape.

When he had finished with the shell, he was about to give it back into Giles's keeping but decided it would be, for the present, safer in his own. In those days pockets in fine clothes were very small, if there were any at all. And the King looked about him for some safer place to carry the shell. Finally he put it into a saddlebag made of cloth of gold that hung upon his horse's snow-white flank. But before he could mount into the saddle, Africa suddenly reared and leapt about in the wildest way.

"Take it out, Your Majesty," cried Giles. "Take the shell out. Someone is talking about your horse and the heat is scaring him!"

"Good Heavens! Does it work with horses too?" said the King. "Yes, it is hot. It must be Hubert, my head groom, talking about you, Africa. The best groom we ever had, eh, my beauty? All he ever talks about is horses. There, there now, no one tried to hurt you. It wouldn't have burned you anyhow, hot as it is. Here, boy: Can I trust you with it again?"

"Yes, indeed, Your Majesty," said Giles. "Have someone give me a pouch string and I'll tie it in my pocket so it cannot shake out, no matter how fast we go."

So the shell was tied tight to Giles and Giles was tied tight to the retainer, and the retainer gripped tight to the horse and off they went once more.

Giles's recollections of this last part of the journey were very broken and jumbled. He remembered more than once being taken down from the horse and the noise of several men talking. Also a hazy blur of moving lanterns and the tossing shadows of horses' heads. And later still he could recall that at one place a great throng of archers and men-at-arms gathered about the party and cheered loudly for the King. From this he guessed sleepily that they were now over the borders of the Duke's lands and safe from capture. But as his weary mind kept dozing off as soon as it had taken in only the half of one idea, he could not tell a very clear or complete story of the strange happenings of that busy night.

The first time that he came fully to his senses, he found himself in new and very wonderful surroundings. He was lying on a silken couch in a very magnificent room. The room, not a large one, was lighted by two candles that flickered in gold candlesticks; and through the partly drawn curtains that covered a long high window, he could see that day was breaking.

He got up. Very stiff he felt. He crossed the room and

looked out. Away down below he saw dimly a beautiful garden, terraces with rose trees, stone walls, and parapets with places cut in them for archers to shoot through. Beyond the garden he could see a great city stretching out a long, long way. Clearly he was in a castle and this room was in one of its high towers. He heard the click of a latch behind him and turned. A serving man was coming in with a tray of food. The man placed the food upon a table and then, almost in a whisper, invited him to sit down and eat. He did so with a good appetite. The man did not leave but remained politely at his elbow to serve him, uncovering one dish after another, pouring out milk for him from a silver jug, and cutting his bread with a large horn-handled knife.

Giles had never been so waited on before and at first he was a little overawed by so much attention. But he was too hungry to have anything spoil his meal, and in a few minutes he had eaten a very hearty breakfast. Then he began asking questions and the man bade him lower his voice. The King, he said, was still asleep in the next room and must not be wakened till the hour was come for the army to march. These rooms, it appeared, were the King's own private apartments. This castle was the chief and most important of all the royal palaces; and this town was the capital, the greatest city in the kingdom.

As the man left by one door, another at the other end of the room opened. And there stood the King, already dressed for riding. Giles guessed that he had, like himself, just lain down for a few hours' rest without taking off his clothes. But he seemed refreshed and in good humor. He asked how Giles had slept and then told him to go back to bed. He hoped to see him again the next day, he said. Giles was about to ask something, but just then he felt the shell burning in his jacket. He took it out to listen. The King, as he crossed the room, paused a moment, watching him.

"It is my mother and father, Your Majesty," said Giles, "and my sister Anne. They are wondering what has become of me. A lame boy, Luke by name, who was very helpful to me in reaching you, has advised them to go into hiding lest they be questioned by the Duke. I beg Your Majesty to let me come with you. I want to see them, to take them the money that they need and set their fears at rest."

"Very good," said the King. "I will be glad to have you with me if you think you can stand the march. You shall ride with my own party as before. But should there be fighting, I may have to send you back here before we reach your home. However, I am in hopes that the Duke's forces will surrender as soon as we lay siege to the town."

"Doesn't Your Majesty want to listen to the shell again before we go?" asked Giles. "You might hear something that would be useful."

The King took it and held it to his ear, listening for a moment.

"The noise, the confusion, are greater than ever," he said. "My own army's talk and turmoil are now added to the Duke's. I can make nothing out clearly and I may not wait, for there is not a moment to lose. I hope to catch the wasps in the nest before they have a chance to get out and sting. Let us be gone. Do you keep the shell. If your lame friend and others know you are with the King, it may be you'll hear news or gossip that will give us better help, even though it be about yourself."

The King then left the room and, with Giles close upon his heels, went clattering down a winding stone staircase that seemed almost to have no bottom. At last it led them out into a wide courtyard. Here in the gray of daybreak were many men and horses. The men, for the most part, were moving swiftly about—almost silently but for a sharp order here and there given in a low voice; while the horses stood waiting, the breath from their nostrils showing plainly in the damp of the early air. Giles was disappointed not to see either his own beautiful Midnight among them, or the King's swift Africa. But instantly he knew that of course they would still be resting from the long march of the day and night before.

In a very few minutes they had mounted new horses, fresh and well groomed. Giles was up behind the same sturdy retainer; and before he put his arms about the man's waist, he made sure that the shell, which was bringing him such strange fortune, was safe in his pocket.

The ride back to Giles's native town was far less exciting than had been the journey away from it. And it did not take nearly so long, for the return was made openly by the best and shortest roads. The King had been very wise in wasting no time. The Duke had not yet had a chance to prepare for any fighting far from his own castle. And the march seemed more like a visiting tour made by the new and well-loved King than anything to do with war. He was greeted and cheered at every hamlet he went through. And if folks wondered at the great masses of archers that went ahead of him and the huge army of men-at-arms that followed him behind, they felt that he had a right to move his troops when and where he wished and bothered their heads no further about it.

Even when the Duke's own lands were entered, things remained very quiet. Guessing that the common people themselves had no knowledge of the plot against them, the King had given the strictest orders that the troops should hurt no one. And not so much as a duck was stolen or an apple picked from the orchards while the King's soldiers passed. Here again no enemy troops were sighted, though Count Godfrey did persuade the King to keep his nobles massed close about him on the march, for fear of a sudden attack from some hidden quarter.

It was when they were within sight of the town, and evening was at hand, that the King at last gave orders for a general halt and called a council of war. All his oldest officers gathered around him while many of the scouts who had been sent ahead were called in.

It was now learned that the Duke and his army were by no means in agreement. His Majesty's sudden march had entirely upset his enemy's plans. The troops that the Duke had ordered out to stop the advance had not been as willing to take up arms against their King as had been expected. For one thing, the Duke had not had time enough to persuade his officers to take part in such rebellion and disloyalty; and for another, his soldiers, seeing this enormous army arriving at their very gates, feared that victory was hardly possible over such a force, all prepared in battle order and so near at hand. For these reasons, the scouts reported, all the Duke's troops had remained within the town, where there was great confusion. Many had already laid down their arms and had sworn they would not fight against the King for anybody or any reward. While the rest were running about within the walls, without leaders or order, wondering what was going to happen next.

When the King heard these things, he sent off Count Godfrey with a few heralds to visit the town and demand its surrender. A full pardon and fair treatment was offered to the common soldiers and the townsfolk, but the Duke and all his relations and attendant nobles were to be put under arrest till they could be tried in the courts of law.

This message was delivered. And within the hour the

heralds came back bearing the town's answer to the King. There was a good deal of surprise when it was noticed that Count Godfrey had not returned with the others. But in his place had come the Mayor, very frightened and upset. He explained that the people had known nothing of the Duke's treacherous plans against the royal person till this morning. They had refused to join in the rebellion. The Duke, in a furious rage, had threatened to hang them all; but had at last decided to take flight while there was still time. Count Godfrey had now gone off in pursuit of him with a picked company of fast horsemen. Order had been restored within the town, and all the Duke's troops had taken the oath of allegiance to the King. The people were now eagerly awaiting His Majesty's arrival that they might have a chance to do him honor and show their loyalty as obedient and loving subjects.

The only reply the King made was to nod his head thoughtfully and to ask after the safety of the Countess Barbara and the others of his party whom he had been forced to leave behind. When the Mayor had assured him that they were all well, His Majesty gave the order to march.

Then the whole of the great army moved on toward the town as darkness settled down upon the land.

CHAPTER EIGHTEEN

THE BOY KNIGHT

His Majesty's second entrance into the town was the grandest thing that Giles had ever seen. The Mayor had sent his own messengers ahead to tell the people of the gracious way in which the King had received him. And long before the army reached the gates, they saw the flare of street bonfires against the sky and heard the pealing of the church bells as the people made ready to welcome the sovereign and his troops. The noise as they drew nearer got louder and louder. And when the royal party passed under the arch of the town gate, it was positively deafening. The people surged forward toward the King, yelling themselves hoarse, waving handkerchiefs and throwing up their caps.

Giles's first thought now was for his own family. And through the smoky light of torches and bonfires, his eyes searched the crowded faces for his parents, Anne, or Luke. He saw nothing of them, however, and he did

not have a chance to dismount till His Majesty had ridden into the courtyard of the castle. Here, where the
noise of the rejoicing townsfolk was not so close and
deafening, the King got down from his horse. He immediately went into the great stone building and the nobles
attendant on him followed.

Giles would have taken this opportunity to slip away,
but as he was still carrying the shell and had not yet
been given permission to leave, he remained at the
King's side. In the great Council Chamber of the Duke's
castle, His Majesty, still dressed in dusty riding clothes,
now held a reception. He sat in the great chair on a
platform at the end of the long room while people in
hundreds came to pay their respects, to be questioned,
or to bring him news.

Giles did not know who most of them were, except
when the heralds announced their names in a loud
voice. First came those of the King's own people who
had been left behind here when he had been forced to
fly. Among them the boy noticed particularly two ladies.
The first was the Princess Sophronia, the King's aunt.
She was very ugly, Giles thought, and made a great fuss
to His Majesty about his leaving her here and the way
she had been treated—though it did not seem, when
she was questioned by her nephew, that she had suf-
fered any very great hardships. The other was a young
girl, the Countess Barbara, who came accompanied by
her father, the Commander of the Scottish Archers. She

had blue eyes and wonderful golden hair. And Giles thought he had never seen anyone so beautiful in his life.

Next to come were some dozens of messengers and officers, who brought reports and news of many matters concerning the town and the dukedom.

Then several men were brought forward under guard with their hands tied behind their backs. These were nobles in the Duke's service who were suspected of being in the plot against the King. His Majesty, with a very black look on his face, questioned them a long time in a quiet voice. He then waved them aside while he gave audience to the others.

The whole business seemed to be taking a long time and the King looked very tired. Giles, hungry for supper and impatient to be off into the town, saw clearly for the first time that being the ruler of a country was not all fun and glory. At last, right at the end of the long line of chamberlains and ministers and whatnot, the Count Godfrey turned up again, his long riding boots spattered with mud, perspiration still dripping from his brow. He seemed almost too weary to stand. The King rose to meet him and bade a servant bring a chair for him. The Count sank down and told his story.

The Duke was dead. He and his brother, with two other leaders in the plot, had been pursued far into the mountains that lay on the south border of the dukedom. There, in a rocky gorge, on the banks of a wide and swiftly running river, Godfrey and his men had cornered him. The Duke, seeing capture at hand, had spurred his horse into the mad torrent, hoping to gain safety on the farther shore. His brother and companions followed him. All four, with their horses, had been swept downstream into the whirlpools and drowned.

When the Count had ended, the King sat for a long time in silence, staring at the floor. At last he looked up and commanded the men who were bound and guarded to be brought again before him.

"Our cousin," said he slowly, "has saved us much trouble. This has been indeed a sad beginning to our reign; but it would have been sadder still if we had had to execute him for treason. And I do not see that any other course would have been left to us had he fallen into our hands. For he was a determined man—and a brave one—even if a traitor to his King. Nor is it our wish that our first days as ruler of the land should be marked in history by bloody penalties and punishments. You gentlemen, by your treason, have deserved to lose your heads. But we judge that you have been led astray by the stronger will of our cousin into a rebellion against us which, if you had been left to yourselves, you would likely never have thought of. As my life has been saved by a boy whom good fortune sent me in the nick of time, so also shall yours be saved by the Duke's unhappy accident. The leader is dead and the rebellion is over. You are pardoned, gentlemen, on the condition of your oath that you will never again go back upon your faith to us and to the Crown."

The ropes about the wrists of the men were loosed, and they at once fell gladly on their knees and swore to be true and faithful to the King and his house for the rest of their days.

His Majesty rose from the great chair with a sigh.

"We now declare the sovereignty of this dukedom," said he, "and our cousin's title with it, at an end forever. Henceforth these lands shall be governed as part of the royal domain and in the same manner as the rest of our kingdom— Where is that boy we brought with us?"

"Do you mean me, sir?" said Giles, popping out from behind the great chair.

His sudden comical appearance changed His Majesty's humor in a flash. The weary seriousness in the King's face turned into an amused smile. It seemed almost as though he grew a little more boyish himself for looking at this lad before him.

"Yes, indeed, I mean you," said he. "What is your name?"

"Giles, Your Majesty."

"Giles? Humph!" muttered the King. "That's not a bad name. He had royal blood in his veins too. He was the patron saint of cripples, wasn't he? . . . That's odd. You spoke of a lame friend you had who helped you in getting to see me. Well, maybe you can carry on Saint Giles's work. Bring your friend to the castle tomorrow.

I'd like to know him. Now, what is your other name? Your family name, I mean."

"Waggonwright, sir."

"Waggonwright— No. I don't like that so well. But never mind. It has an honest sound. Does your father make wagons?"

"Yes, Your Majesty. He was once master of the biggest workshop in this town. But bad times came upon him and his trade has dwindled down to almost nothing."

"Yes, yes," said the King. "I remember you told me. Don't let me forget to send him the money I promised. How old are you?"

"Nine and three quarters, Your Majesty."

"Do you know what a knight is?"

"Yes, sir."

"Well, Giles, I'm going to make you into a knight. It's all against the rules and customs at your age. But I'm going to make you one just the same—for your bravery in the service of the Crown."

"Bravery, Your Majesty?" asked Giles with a puzzled look on his face. "What bravery?"

"Didn't you risk your silly little neck jumping in front of my horse? You nearly got skewered in a half a dozen places."

"I don't believe I'd have dared if it hadn't been for Luke, sir," murmured Giles.

"Well, and if it hadn't been for you, young man, I wouldn't be standing here now. Godfrey, lend me your sword."

The Count stepped forward, unbuckled his belt, and held out his sword hilt within reach. The King drew the bright, shiny blade out of the scabbard and turned again to Giles.

"Kneel down, boy," said he. "Don't be alarmed. We're not going to chop your head off. This is just the ceremony we have to go through."

Giles dropped on his right knee and bowed his head. He felt the sword touch him lightly on the shoulder and he heard the King say solemnly: "Arise, *Sir* Giles."

He got up wondering if he were dreaming. But even while he wondered, the King spoke to him again.

"Sir Giles Waggonwright," said he, "we wish to attach you to the Royal Household. Some duty must be found for you. Now tell me: What can you do best?"

Sir Giles scratched his head in a most unknightly fashion and a very blank look came over his face.

"I'm afraid I—er—hardly know, Your Majesty," he stammered.

"Come now," said the King. "We can all do some things better than others. Think. Think hard."

For a full half minute Giles thought hard. Then his face brightened with a new thought.

"I'm very good at finding things, Your Majesty," said he. "My mother always sets me hunting when she loses her thimble. And my father, if he mislays a chisel or a hammer, always calls on me to get it for him. Indeed, he has often said I never was good for anything but finding."

A quiet titter of amusement ran through the courtiers that stood about the King. But His Majesty clapped his hands and almost shouted: "*Finding*, did you say? How splendid! That's the very thing. It couldn't be better. Because, do you know what I am best in? Losing things. I lose everything. Papers, letters, riding whips, dogs, gloves, hats, books, everything. So, you shall be the King's Finder."

His Majesty raised his hand for attention. Everyone stopped whispering and no sound disturbed the silence in the long room.

"We wish," said he, "to create a new office in the Royal Household. It is to be known as the King's Finder and shall, in order of honor and precedence, come between that of the Chief Equerry and the Keeper of the Great Seal. This young knight, Sir Giles Waggonwright, shall be the first to hold it. Please see," he added to one of the messengers at hand, "that the Lord Chamberlain is notified of the appointment as soon as possible."

The King then declared the audience at an end. And everyone gladly followed him out into the dining hall of the castle, where a grand supper had been prepared for the whole company.

The next day Giles's family was brought to the palace by royal command. Anne, with her father and mother, was quite overcome by the sudden dazzling importance that surrounded her brother, the boy-knight. They were most graciously treated as the private guests of His Majesty and took lunch with the King himself. The father was presented with the money that had been promised, enough to pay all his debts and to make a new start in business besides. The King asked Giles's mother for permission to take her son with him to his capital beyond the mountains, promising to look after him well and to allow him to visit his family whenever he wished. He wanted to take Anne also, to be a maid of honor to the Queen Dowager, his own mother. But the parents could not bear to be parted from both their children at once, and it was agreed that perhaps later, when Anne was older, she should be sent to join her brother in the Royal Household.

Luke, too, turned up a little later and was brought to see the King. For fear of arrest he had been keeping out of the way till he had heard of the Duke's flight. Giles was indeed glad to see his friend again and asked that he might be taken too. So the King appointed him as esquire to Giles himself. It seemed that all knights had one esquire at least in their service; and thus Luke joined the royal retinue as right-hand man to the King's Finder.

Giles asked the lame boy if he had seen or heard anything of Agnes the Applewoman. But he could give no news of her. And though the Haunted Inn was searched again from cellar to attic, and Giles kept the King's shell constantly in his pocket, hoping to hear her speak of him, no word of her, of where she had gone or what she was doing, could be learned. And they were forced for the present to give up hope of reaching her. Giles was sorry about this, because he wanted the King to meet her also.

"You know, Luke," he said, "I think His Majesty should have her, too, in his service. He needs clever people. And, after all, she is the one who should be thanked for everything—even the King's safety. For it was she who gave us the shell and told us what it could do. Do you suppose that wretched Duke did her some mischief before he took to flight?"

"No, I don't believe so," said Luke. "I fancy I'd have heard of it if she had been taken. What I think is that she is more scared than ever of being charged with witchcraft. You see, now that she has made me completely well when I was supposed to be a hopeless cripple, they'd likely say that she had used some magic on me or performed some trick with the Devil's help."

Then, for the first time since he had seen his friend again, Giles noticed that he no longer carried a crutch.

"Oh, Luke!" he cried. "Can you use both your legs now?"

Luke drew himself up squarely on both feet, firm and even.

"I'm a whole man now, Giles." He laughed. "I haven't used the crutch since I lost it. It was when you leapt out to give the King the shell. I lost it between the legs of that soldier who was going to strike you down. Then I ran like the mischief down the street lest I'd be caught by the guard. And I never noticed that I had used both legs—nor even thought of the crutch I'd left behind—till I reached a hiding place."

For a moment Giles stared dumbfounded at the happy face and the strong and healthy figure of his once lame friend. Then he murmured as if to himself: " 'Giles, the patron saint of cripples,' that's what the King said. It was after him that I was named. Yet it was Agnes that did it, Agnes the Applewoman—Shragga the Witch! Listen, Luke, do you think maybe she is a saint instead of a witch, a saint in some disguise—perhaps the Patron Giles himself?"

"I don't know. Who can tell?" said Luke thoughtfully. "She used nothing but her hands, twisting and pulling at my knee. I'm sorry we can't find her now. I did so want to thank her—to have her see me run without a crutch."

"Well," said Giles with a sigh, "maybe she'll turn up again some day. She does, you know, in the most unexpected places."

"And always where she's needed," Luke added with a nod.

"It's late," said Giles. "Let us get to bed now. We need rest. For tomorrow, Luke, we set out for the capital and fortune—tomorrow we ride with the King!"

BOOK II

CHAPTER ONE

THE KING'S FINDER

And so the next day Giles started out for the capital; and with his starting out there began for him a new life, the life of palaces and princes.

He never thought that it would be nine whole years, from that morning, before he would return to his father's town. Yet so it was to be. It was not that he had no wish to come back. Indeed, he often planned to do so. But something always came along to prevent it. For his own life was a very busy and a very happy one; and in those nine years many strange happenings took up his thoughts and filled his days.

It must be said in Giles's favor that he did not allow all the new splendor and glory to turn his head. Which was very remarkable in one so young. For it became quite clear to everyone as soon as the King got back to his court that the boy he had brought with him stood very high in the royal favor. Not only was the young knight, with his one esquire, given rooms in the King's own apartments, but it was noticed that the King took him with him wherever he went. More than that, His Majesty, it seemed, often talked over important business of state with him—even before taking advice from his regular councilors and ministers; and he was always giving the boy important tasks to carry out.

And before long Giles was surprised to find that all manner of grand and high persons about the court were most anxious to gain his favor and show great friendliness to him. Hoping to get him to put in a good word for them and their affairs with the King, they even tried to give him presents. That was how he came to be spoken of sometimes in the history of this particular king's reign as the "Boy Chancellor." For even princes of foreign lands who wanted to make treaties and trade agreements with this country sent secret messengers to Giles with gorgeous gifts before they made their business known to the King himself.

Among the grand folk who sought to gain the favor of the King's Finder, there was His Majesty's own aunt, the Princess Sophronia. Giles found this lady to be most peculiar. Not only was she a fussbudget and dreadfully ugly, but she was also very vain, thinking herself a great beauty. She was no longer young either. Yet she expected to marry an emperor, or some important sovereign at least. And at first Giles wondered why. But he soon saw the reason for it. Because she was the King's aunt, many of the people about the court flattered her no end and were always telling her how beautiful and noble she was and that she ought surely some day to be the queen of a great country. This was the first time that Giles came to see how some persons about the courts of kings were not to be trusted, that many who pretended to be loyal friends were nothing but double-faced, selfish schemers.

The poor King could not abide his Aunt Sophronia; yet because she was of the blood royal, he had to be polite to her. And she was forever pestering him for all manner of favors and complaining of this and that. Here, too, Giles came in very handy to his master. Whenever His Majesty saw the Princess coming, he would whisper: "Here comes my aunt. For pity's sake, keep her talking for me while I slip away into the garden."

And so Sir Giles Waggonwright, the King's Finder, had to have many conversations with the Princess Sophronia and got to know Her Highness very well. But he soon saw that he had to keep her and many others in their places. He politely refused to annoy the King with most of their worrisome requests and plans, and he would not take the presents and bribes of money with which they tempted him to carry their prayers to the sovereign.

Among the people at the court, however, there were two who never bothered the King's Finder to do things for them—though both of them were indeed good friends of his. One was the Queen Dowager, His Majesty's mother. Till the King should get himself a wife, his mother still held the position of Queen, as she had done when his father was alive. She was a very kind little old lady with merry twinkling eyes and was beloved by everyone throughout the realm. The other was the beautiful Countess Barbara, daughter of the Commander of the Scottish Archers.

This girl, although she was still very young, seemed to grow more lovely with every passing year, and princes and rulers from many lands had already asked for her hand. Marriages were arranged very early in life in those days, and after the betrothal an engagement was sometimes announced long before the wedding. The Countess was now a lady-in-waiting to the Queen Dowager. But she did not as yet appear to be interested in the idea of marrying. She seemed to have no time or liking for the noble youths who fluttered around the King's mother, living in the hope that the beautiful Barbara might some day cast favorable eyes on them. Indeed, Giles often thought she cared very little at all for any part of the grand and gossipy and ceremonious life of the court. She loved the countryside and the common people of the land, dogs and horses, gardens and fields.

The King himself was this way inclined also—as were Giles and Luke. The business of reigning was indeed a business for the poor King. He had to attend to it and he did. But he was always glad to throw aside the pomp and grandeur and go off with no other attendants but the Countess, Giles, and Luke, picnicking in the country. Here the four of them had a grand time, climbing trees, racing their dogs, jumping their horses over hedge and stream, gathering blackberries and lunching off sandwiches and hard-boiled eggs. These doings sometimes caused a good deal of talk among the ministers and important persons at the court, who did not feel that His Majesty always behaved with proper kingly dignity.

The thought often came to Giles that although the beautiful Barbara was not in the least interested in love, perhaps the King was very much interested in Barbara—if he were not actually in love with her.

When Giles had first come to the palace and was dressed by the court tailors, measured by the royal saddlers, given a whole suite of rooms of his own, and treated with all the honor and respect due to a knight, he had been a little anxious and afraid. His fear was that he might not, after all this trouble had been taken over him, prove to be such a wonderful finder as he had boasted of being.

But he very soon made good his claim. He certainly had a gift for finding things—and the King had an even greater gift for losing them. Most of the other officers of the Royal Household were held strictly to certain regulations, and they had fixed hours when they must wait upon the King with exact and solemn ceremony. But with Giles it was very different. He had no set hours for his work and attendance. And if this kept him busier than the others, he at all events had the consolation of being free. Special orders were given by His Majesty that the King's Finder should be supplied with keys to every door and gate in the castle, and that he was to be admitted to any room at any hour whatever. This came in very handy for Giles when he had a fancy to get a piece of pie from the castle pantry in the middle of the night. But it also caused some inconvenience to others, as, for instance, when he woke the Princess Sophronia out of a sound sleep at two o'clock in the morning to see if she had borrowed a book which the King had missed.

Yes, the King's habit of losing things certainly kept the Finder busy. Often there were two or more things lost in one day and Giles wouldn't know which to hunt for first. But after a while he saw that his hardest tasks always came whenever the King left his private rooms. So long as the thing lost lay in the royal apartments, Giles knew he did not have to go far to seek it. But when His Majesty wandered off into the country and left his best jacket hanging on a tree because the day was warm, the matter was not so easy.

So Giles formed the habit of always watching the King to see if he laid things down in the wrong places and, when possible, of slipping them into his own pockets so as to have them ready when his master needed them again. He had a tremendous memory for this sort of work, and with practice it grew better and better. Sometimes, when he appeared to be giving his whole attention to someone else, the Finder was watching the King out of the corner of his eye; and if His Majesty threw a letter aside carelessly or, unthinking, slipped his favorite pen into a drawer, Giles could tell him weeks or months afterward just where he had left it.

Other tricks he used to help him in his findings, but they were nearly all some form of what is called observation, keeping the eyes open, noticing little things. Often he would question the King as to where he saw the missing article last. And when he had found that out, he would ask him to remember what he had done minute by minute, and where he had been, foot by foot, since. This often took hours and wearied the King not a little; but in the end Giles nearly always knew to a yard or so just where to go and look for what had been lost.

Two very famous cases showing the cleverness of the King's Finder are mentioned in the history of this country. One was when a shoe of the King's disappeared mysteriously from the royal bedchamber. The King did not care anything about the shoe, but he was much upset at losing the buckle on it, which was one of a very precious gold pair that had belonged to his father. Everyone suspected the grooms of the bedchamber of having stolen it. But Giles thought otherwise. It seemed likely to him that if a servant had done it, he would have taken both the shoes and not one only.

So he went to see the Keeper of the Royal Kennels and asked if there was any puppies there. The Keeper said yes, one of the greyhounds had a litter about five weeks old, but the mother was in a terrible state because one of the pups was missing since last night. Giles then put the mother on a leash and led her to the King's bedchamber. Here she got more excited and restless than ever, and picking up the scent of her young one, she dragged Giles after her out of the castle and down to the far end of an orchard. She stopped at the mouth of a deep pit which was used for throwing leaves and rubbish in. The puppy, worn out with his long journey, was found asleep at the bottom of it. And beside him was the King's shoe, nearly chewed in halves, but with the precious buckle still safely sewed to it.

The other exploit, which made the Finder even more famous in the story and legend of the kingdom, threw almost a mysterious glory and respect around his name. Some of the courtiers who had grown jealous of the power and importance of the boy-knight sought to destroy his favor with the King and hatched a plot against him. Up to this time Giles's success had been simply marvelous. Not a thing of value which he had set out to seek had he failed to find. Their idea was to make him fail in order that the King would lose faith in him. So one night they managed to get hold of some of the crown jewels and hid them in different places in the castle garden. And after they had carefully covered up all their traces, they waited to see what would happen.

As soon as the loss of the jewels became known, the whole palace was thrown into a great state of excitement. Again several persons were accused of theft or carelessness, and again the King's Finder was called in to solve the mystery. After questioning those whose business it was to guard such things, Giles did a little thinking. He knew almost at once that this could not be the work of any ordinary robber from outside. And if it had been done by anybody inside the castle, he guessed it was a trap laid for the purpose of injuring himself and his reputation—also that more than one person was likely engaged in the business. So the first thing he did was to warn the King that he must be patient, because this piece of work might take a little time.

Part of Sir Giles's duties as an officer of the Royal Household was that of guardian and keeper of the Whispering Shell. Hardly anyone around the court knew of the existence of this shell. The King had been anxious to keep its powers a secret. Giles nearly always carried it upon his person, to be ready to hand it to the King anytime he asked for it. And whenever the Finder left it behind him, he locked it in a special strong cupboard in his rooms, to which only himself and the King had a key.

Once he had made up his mind that several people were in the plot, he kept the shell near him day and night. Even when sleeping he put it next to his cheek upon the pillow so that its heat should wake him up if anyone spoke of him. About one o'clock in the morning on the third day after the jewels vanished, he woke up with a great start. The shell was burning away like mad, which meant, he knew, that several people were speaking of him at once. He rolled over and clapped it to his ear.

"Drat the country brat!" said a voice. "This will queer him with the King—or I'm a Turk. 'King's Finder' indeed! He'll have to be the Devil's own finder to root out the piece I buried. Two feet down under the flagstones of the East Pavilion, I laid it—and everything put back so a mole couldn't tell I'd been there. Pass around that bottle of wine again and we'll drink to his disgrace and destruction."

"Sir Giles Waggonwright!" sneered another voice. "What a name! And whoever heard of making a knight of a boy that age? How old is he now? Sixteen. Huh! And when he was raised to the nobility, he was not yet ten. The King must have been mad—bringing a workman's boy to the palace to lord it over his betters. Well, we'll see the end of him soon now. A whole lifetime couldn't be long enough to discover *my* hiding place. The Coronation Ring—with the Persian Emerald—it's under a fathom of mud in the Turtle Pool. Let us see if his cheeky little peasant nose can dig *that* out. May the plague rot him!"

Then a third voice joined in—a fourth. And a fifth. The rattle of wine cups. Curses and laughter.

For a full half hour the talk went on and Giles listened. Although no names were mentioned, he recognized every voice. And before the shell grew cold, he had learned where each one of the boasting courtiers had hidden his part of the treasure.

The dawn was just breaking as Giles, with Luke behind him, slipped out into the castle garden. They stopped a moment at the gardener's toolhouse, which was quickly opened with the Finder's passkeys.

And when the King a few hours later sat down to breakfast in his rooms, there lay all the missing jewels upon the table before him.

His Majestry tried hard to make Giles tell how and where he had discovered them. But the Finder begged to be allowed to keep his secret.

"Very good, Giles," he said at last, smiling. "So long as you stay in my service, I am content. For truly I believe that so long as I have you, I need not worry if I lose my crown and kingdom. Sit down and have some eggs with me."

And so out of this plot against him came nothing but greater fame for Giles; and the Lord Treasurer was ordered to add another hundred crowns to the yearly wage of the King's Finder.

But the five courtiers, whenever they passed him in the corridors and passages of the palace, quickly looked the other way and would not meet his eye. And before long they asked the royal permission to travel for their health, and they left the King's court, never to return again.

CHAPTER TWO

THE FRIENDSHIP THAT DOES NOT BETRAY

But Giles did not make many enemies; in fact, those five courtiers who tried to disgrace him could be said to be almost the only ones he had. On the other hand, he had a great number of very good friends. These were not by any means all picked from among the great. With the freedom which his peculiar duties gave him, he was able to chat and hobnob with whom he chose. In that he was like the King himself, who was perhaps the only other person at the court who did not have to be careful about his dignity with those beneath him in station. Thus the two had many strange friends in common.

One of these was the Chief of the Royal Cooks. He was a monstrously fat man with a very jolly face which looked as though it was made from well-tanned leather. Both Giles and the King used to visit his kitchen at any odd hour of the day, not only to enjoy his excellent pastries and sweetmeats but also to listen to his ridicu-

lously funny stories. He had been in charge of the palace
kitchen long before the King was born and had prepared
his porridge for him when he was a baby. He had an
enormous memory, which, in spite of his being sixty
years of age, only seemed to remember the merry things
in life and to forget the sad ones.

Another of their queer friends was a gardener. That
is, he was a gardener when he was in the King's service.
What he was at other times no one knew. He was something of a mystery. And he was known as Geoffrey the
Gypsy. It was never proved that he was a real Gypsy—
nor, certainly, was he a regular gardener. There was
nothing regular about him. It was said that he, too, had
first been brought into the royal service in the days of
the King's father, whose great hobby had been raising
roses—white ones in particular. In searching his country
for people skilled in rose culture, the old King had come
upon Geoffrey somewhere and set him to work in his
gardens. He quickly proved himself to be such a wizard
with the flowers that he became quite an important person, and his royal master gave him all sorts of liberties
and special privileges not granted to his other servants.

The young King always remembered his father with
a very real love and admiration. And he wished that the
palace rosaries should be kept up in the best possible
state in memory of him. And so even now the queer
Geoffrey (who was sometimes spoken of as the "Rose
Doctor") was often still to be seen dreamily pottering

around the terraces on the south slope of the castle hill, a pruning knife or trowel in his hand—and always alone. For the other gardeners at the castle would have nothing to do with him, nor he with them. But he never stayed for long. Some strange wandering call seemed to be forever tugging at his heart. And sooner or later he would come to the King and say: "Your Majesty, I've got to go."

The King always expected this. And without argument he would let him depart, quite sure that in his own mysterious way the Gypsy would know when the roses needed him again and would return in time, of his own accord. Geoffrey was strangely well read for a man of his kind. He seemed to know most of the Greek and Latin poets by heart and was full of a great knowledge of life, which gripped the young minds of the King and his Finder by its unboasting but fearless honesty. Hours and hours they spent with him while he trained the ramblers, chatting of everything under heaven, from moles and marriages to music and the siege of Troy.

Geoffrey was a great enemy of war. And he was always looking forward to the day when it and its unjust evils should pass from the world forever. This, in those times when men still thought that killing was the greatest if not the only work of heroes, was brave and independent thinking. Especially when spoken out before a prince who kept a large army of his own. And long afterward Giles often wondered how much the Gypsy's words shaped the thoughts and ambitions of the King. For the time came when the people looked back upon the days of this young man's kindly rule and spoke of them, with a sigh of reverence, as the Reign of Peace.

It would seem surprising perhaps that the King did not more often carry the Whispering Shell himself. But, as he had found when it was first given him, it was, during the ordinary hours of the day, almost worthless for his own use. The great number of voices all over his kingdom—and outside his boundaries as well—all talking about him at once made a babel that no one could understand. It was therefore at nighttime, when most folk were asleep, that Giles brought the shell to the royal apartments. There, with the cares of state over for the day, the King would listen in comfort to learn if any stayed awake to talk about him.

Sometimes he would hear nothing of importance, would lay it aside and, after a game of chess with Giles, retire to bed. And other times he would hear disturbing voices of evil, more and still more of these everlasting plottings within his kingdom. These messages would often force him to have someone imprisoned, punished, or banished from the realm. The hours of darkness are the time when envious men get together to hatch plots. And many a night he swore to Giles that he would one day smash the shell to atoms and forever silence its whisperings of treachery and ill faith. But then when he heard something that helped him in the good government of his kingdom, he would change his mind about this powerful, mysterious thing that had come to him out of the sea.

Once or twice he heard of coming wars. The voices of other kings in the neighboring realms talking with their ministers and commanders, discussing whether they should, or should not, take up arms against him. Here the shell played a peculiar part. For it allowed him to see through other eyes into the causes of war, the things that led up to suffering and death for thousands, growing in the minds of men who lived, as it were, with the right hand always on the sword hilt. And to this young prince, whose greatest wish was to keep peace and happiness always in the lives of his people, it seemed almost as if he were himself far away in those foreign kingdoms, present there, taking part in the arguments he listened to. Often he saw justice in what these men of the other side had to say. And sometimes he heard their plans of battle and arrangements for attacking his borders. And that was partly the reason that he was able to become a preventer, rather than a maker, of wars.

One afternoon Giles, in spite of all his care to keep the shell from the eyes and knowledge of the court, had a curious accident. He was sitting in one of the garden pavilions, where he thought no one would be likely to disturb him, listening to the shell himself. He was hoping to hear word of his sister and parents, whom he had not seen for a very long time. Suddenly the Princess

Sophronia appeared at the door. She saw he held a shell to his ear, and before he had time to stuff it in his pocket, she grabbed it from him and listened to it herself. She expected, of course, to hear nothing but the roaring of the sea. But as luck would have it, two people in the castle were talking of her that very moment. One was her own lady's maid and the other was a groom attached to a foreign prince who was visiting the castle at the time. This prince, it was said, was going to marry the Princess Sophronia. And because it now seemed likely that she would someday be queen of a big country, many people about the court were saying more flattering things about her than usual. The groom wanted to marry the Princess's lady's maid, hoping it would help him on in the world. He was saying at this moment: "When that most gracious, generous, beautiful, and noble lady, your mistress, the Princess Sophronia, is wedded to my master, would it not be indeed fitting that you marry me so that we may live together in the same country?"

At that the King's aunt closed her eyes and purred with delight. For to this empty-headed woman, flattery of any kind was the breath of life. Then, without another word to Giles, she departed, taking the shell with her.

But she had not reckoned on the peculiar duties and liberties of the King's Finder. That night Giles waited outside her bedroom door till he heard the Princess snoring. Then he went in and removed the shell from beneath her pillow without waking her.

Next day she came and indignantly accused him of stealing it from her. With polite respect he told her that it was His Majesty's property and he had been bound, as the King's Finder, to get it and take it back.

But Sophronia was a determined if not a beautiful princess. She stuck to Giles for hours, begging and demanding that he give it to her. He became afraid that she might go talking and complaining about it all over the castle. Therefore he struck a bargain with her. He said the King had spoken lately once or twice of someday not wanting the shell anymore. So if she would swear to keep it a secret, and it was still unbroken when the King had done with it, he would promise it would be hers.

The time came much sooner than he expected when he had to make good this promise.

That same night Giles took a late supper with the King in his apartments, as he often did. When the dishes had been cleared away, the King asked for the shell and held it to his ear. Presently Giles left him for a moment to go and speak to Luke. And when he returned, the shell was on the table and the King was marching back and forth like a caged lion.

"Why, Your Majesty," Giles began, "what has—"

"Oh, don't 'majesty' me!" yelled the King. "We don't stand on ceremony here. Majesty! I wish I'd never heard the word. I wish I'd been born poor, like you, Giles. At least you've never had people plotting against you all your life. Lying to your face and scheming behind your back—scheming to kill you like a dog! And my own flesh and blood it is, my own flesh and blood, hoping, wishing, praying for my death. Prayers for His Majesty the King! That's what I heard first. The monks over in the abbey at their midnight devotions. Then this. More prayers for the King! Hah! Hah! Hah! Prayers for the King's *death!* My own flesh and blood—and a woman at that—praying someone to stick a knife in my ribs!"

He dropped onto a couch and ran his fingers through his hair like one distraught.

"It's too much, Giles," he groaned presently. "I can't bear it anymore. I can never listen again. Let them come and slaughter me, here, in my sleep if they will. But I'll listen to no more plots from them and lie awake nights wondering whether I should behead them before they murder me. Who can I trust? Tell me, who?"

The King's voice rose again to something near a shriek. "*Who?* You, my mother, Barbara, and Luke. Who else? No one."

Giles moved forward to say something. But the King's voice ran on again brokenly, madly. His hand suddenly shot out, pointing to the table.

"And there lies the trouble, Giles: the shell! It has robbed me of my faith in all. When shall I find peace again? Kill it! Take that battle-ax from off the wall— behind you. Smash it! There's a curse in it! Smash it into powder, I tell you!"

Giles hesitated a moment, trying to find words to soothe the wildness of his master's mood. Then in a flash the King leapt up, snatched the shell off the table, and hurled it with all his might through the open window of the tower. With a great sigh he dropped down upon the sofa again, and a sudden calm came upon him, as though he had at last rid himself of something evil.

But the keen ears of the King's Finder were listening. Listening for a distant crash. The night was still. He knew that if the shell fell into the courtyard from that tremendous height, it would be broken in a thousand pieces. If, on the other hand, the King's raving strength had thrown it farther still, it would fall into the garden, where the softness of flower beds, moss, or turf might save it from destruction. It would take some seconds to fall, Giles told himself. And as he waited in the silent room, he found he was thinking of Agnes. Were the shell destroyed, it would be for the best; if it was saved, it would mean its work was not yet done.

And then, still listening for the answer to the question in his mind, he suddenly knew that he had waited overlong—past the time for it to fall. It *had* dropped into the garden—without a sound.

Giles moved over to the bowed figure sitting on the couch.

"Your Maj—" he began and then checked himself. He laid his arm across the King's shoulders.

"Good friend," he whispered gently, "some people

you will always have about you whom you can trust, and no man these days can boast of more than that. Remember them; forget the others. Get you to bed now and rest safe—safe in the friendship that does not betray. By your leave we will dismiss the grooms. And Luke and I will sleep across the threshold of your door."

CHAPTER THREE

GEOFFREY THE GYPSY

The King never spoke of the shell again, nor did he ever tell what member of his family he had heard speaking that night. It is likely, however, that he took some steps to protect himself against the plot, because nothing ever came of it. He was not destined (as were so many of his line before him) for a death by violence.

The next morning Giles was up early. But he made no sound. He was standing motionless at the open window while he waited for his sleeping master to stir. He was reminded of his first awakening in this castle, years before, as he gazed down over the palace courtyard, the sloping gardens, and the great city beyond, all murky and dim in the half-light of dawn.

Presently he noticed someone moving among the flowers and bushes below. It was Geoffrey the Gypsy with a spade upon his shoulder. A moment later the figure paused, standing now, Giles calculated, at just about the spot where the shell would have fallen last night. Geoffrey stooped and picked something up from the ground. And the Finder suddenly leaned out over the sill, screwing up his eyes as if to make out what manner of thing it was. But at that moment the King stirred upon the bed, turning with a sleepy sigh. At once Giles left the window and came noiselessly to his master's side.

Later in the morning he took a stroll through the garden. By now the sun was well risen and the warm, bright air was sweet with the scent of flowers. He sought out the Gypsy and found him grubbing at the roots of a white rose.

"Did you happen to find anything around here this morning?"

"Why, yes" answered the gardener, straightening up. "A shell. I was wondering how it got here."

He wiped earthy hands upon his apron, stepped over to his jacket, which hung from the limb of a tree, and drew the shell from the pocket.

"It's a beauty," he said as he held it out.

"Thank you." Giles took it and instantly turned to go.

But after a few steps along the terrace, the King's Finder bethought him he had perhaps been a little ungracious. The Gypsy, with whom he nearly always spent a minute chatting when he met him, might even think himself suspected of keeping something not his own. Giles did not want to talk about the shell to

Geoffrey—who of course could not know anything of its strange powers. But he would not have him offended for the world. He turned and came back to the stooping gardener.

"Do you believe in magic, Geoffrey?" he asked, plucking a sprig of lavender from a bush that overhung the path.

"Why—er—yes," said the Gypsy, "if by that you mean, sir, anything we can't understand or explain. But don't forget, a whole lot passes for magic with us which is simple enough to birds and beasts. Every day something we thought had the Devil in it is shown to be naught more than our own simpleminded ignorance. 'Must be magic,' says man as soon as he grows tired of trying to understand a thing. Like children! What's more magic than the way a flower grows out of a seed, I'd like to know?"

And then, to Giles's great astonishment, the gardener looked straight at him and added: "Were you thinking of that shell, sir, by any chance?"

Giles could not yet decide how much the man knew. The jacket had been hanging on a tree six paces away.

"Er—yes; I was," he said at last.

"Oh, well, I've seen lots stranger things than that in foreign lands. Queer deeds—where a man couldn't believe his own eyes. Yet there they were, happening in front of him."

The frown deepened on the face of the King's Finder.

Suddenly he stepped forward and lowered his voice.

"Do you mean to tell me, Geoffrey, you knew about the shell? How—it—er—"

"How it whispers?" put in the gardener as the other hesitated. "Grows hot when others speak of you? Yes, sir. I was listening to it a few minutes before you came along."

He turned back to his work on the rose tree. Giles could not make him out at all.

"You meant to keep it, then?" he asked at last, glancing at the jacket on the tree limb.

"No, indeed. What would I want it for? To hear people talk about me? No. People have to talk, sir. And if they want to talk about me, let 'em, I say. But *listen* to them?" A smile came over the Gypsy's calm, lean face. "I've spent a lot of time, sir, lying in meadows watching the clouds sail over me, changing their drifting shapes. But I haven't got time for listening to folks chatter about me. If I could hear 'em talk of someone else, or tell stories or something, maybe 'twould be different."

"Were you, then, going to sell it for money?"

"Money, sir?" The gardener shook his head. "No. The King's wage is enough for all I need."

He drew a pruning knife from his belt and cut a faded bloom from the white rose tree.

"Well, what *did* you mean to do with it, then?" asked Giles. "You had put it in your pocket."

"I was going to grow ferns in it, sir. It would look

elegant in the rockery behind the Queen's bench—with maidenhair and maybe myrtle. I'd planned to set it there when I was done with the roses. But if you want it, sir, of course that's—"

Geoffrey the Gypsy gazed after the young knight, who had suddenly walked away from him down the terrace. He put his pruning knife back in his sheath and went to work again with the spade.

"Drat these moles!" he muttered.

But as he bent over the fresh-turned earth, he did not see that the King's Finder had halted again—this time at a distant bend in the terrace—and was now gazing back at him.

Giles was accustomed to find himself in thoughtful mood when he had come to the end of a talk with Geoffrey. But this calm and sunny morning he felt more stirred and uneasy in his heart than he had ever been before. He wondered why he had broken off the chat and hurried away. And then, with sudden queer shame, he knew he had been afraid—afraid lest when he had done cross-questioning Geoffrey, the Gypsy would turn and ask him what *he* meant to do with the shell.

He had come out this morning to get it for the Princess Sophronia. Now that the King was done with it, he must make good his promise, and she should be allowed to listen to all the praise and flattery she could get. He found that he had to take it from a Gypsy gardener to carry it to a princess royal. And he did not like his mission at all. Those smooth-tongued courtiers, he thought to himself, would have said that he was taking it from the lowliest in the land to the highest. But as he looked back, that peaceful figure delving in the earth about the roses suddenly seemed to grow and grow against the sky—taller, stronger, and more lasting than the towering castle itself. And when he put the shell in his pocket and turned to go on, Giles knew in his own heart that he was really taking it from the greatest to the smallest.

At the foot of the stone steps leading up to the courtyard, his mood was pleasantly changed by his meeting with the Countess Barbara. She was close to his own age of eighteen years, shorter than he but tall for a girl, graceful and slender. And Giles was reminded of the white roses he had just left as she smiled down a greeting to him. She was on her way, with two frisky black spaniels, to get water lilies for the Queen Mother from the Lower Lake. Giles begged her to wait for him a moment while he did an errand. She said she would if he would not be too long.

He dashed into the castle and up the great stairs to the Princess's rooms.

Sophronia's joy at getting the shell for her own at last seemed to Giles almost sad as she grabbed it from his hand with a happy squeal. Of late she had been growing a little hard of hearing, and in her fumbling eagerness to see if it still worked, she nearly dropped it more than once. But at last she got it, growing warm already, to her ear. She heard the foreign prince—the one she hoped to marry—telling the Queen Mother that no stars in the heavens were so beautiful or bright as the eyes of his beloved Sophronia. (What the prince was really thinking was that no coins would look so beautiful or bright as the dowry money he hoped to get from the King when he married his pest of an aunt. But he didn't say that, so it didn't spoil the Princess's joy.)

And when Giles left her and went running down the steps to the Countess Barbara, the romantic Sophronia was seated at the window with the cold shell still clutched to her ear, smilingly waiting for more.

CHAPTER FOUR

AT THE LOWER LAKE

The Lower Lake was one of the most beautiful parts of the castle grounds. It, too, had been dear to the heart of the old King, the lover of gardens, who had himself seen to its laying out with the help of a landscape architect very famous in his day. It had been purposely left quite wild in order that the waterfowl and the deer from the game park should make of it a place of quiet and safe retreat. In the center of a wide meadow, edged with bullrushes, patched with lily pads, its clear waters reflected the moods of the sky—and sometimes the images of peacefully dabbling diver ducks or the handsome antlers of a drinking stag. And often when stormy weather drove the bird life inland from the sea, its ruffled surface was alive with wild geese, gathered there as the old King planned they should, to enjoy the protection and hospitality of a royal estate.

But today, arriving at its sedgy banks, Giles and the

Countess Barbara found not a ripple to disturb its calm blue mirror, asleep beneath a cloudless, windless heaven. This quiet did not last for long, however, for the spaniels, Maggie and Mollie, soon scented out an otter from the osiers at the north end. And in a moment the two dogs were thrashing about in the water in boisterous and vain pursuit.

From the shore, with the aid of hooked hazel poles, plenty of lilies could be gathered without wading. And it took Giles barely fifteen minutes to collect more than an armful for Barbara to take back to the Queen. The two then fell to throwing sticks into the water for the spaniels to fetch. This grew into a sort of game, Giles betting on Mollie and Barbara on Maggie, to see which was the faster swimmer.

It was a keen and hard-fought, splashy battle. But in the end Maggie proved herself the champion beyond all doubt or question. And presently Barbara said it was time to return to the castle.

But Giles did not want the game to end. On the way here the Countess had seemed a trifle sad and serious. The play with the dogs had cheered her up. A healthy flush had now come into her cheeks and a livelier sparkle to her glorious blue eyes. She was standing by the bank gathering the lilies one by one into her arms. Their wet red stems glistened in her slender, well-shaped fingers. Behind her rose the wonderful sweep of the castle hill, dotted with clumps of oaks, topped by the gray

towers of the King's palace. And again, as when he had first seen her, Giles thought that surely the world never held a creature of more grace or fairer beauty.

Even when she spoke again of going, he was trying to think of some excuse to keep her. With her, out here in the sun, amid all the gracious peace of the Lower Lake, he would ask nothing better than to stay for—well, he didn't know or care how long. Might he not so perhaps hold that gayer sparkle in her eyes? They had known each other many years now, yet they seemed never to have talked of anything but dogs and horses, country things—seldom of people or life.

His own mood at the time puzzled Giles a lot. He asked himself: Is this beautiful, strange girl happy? *He* felt happy. And he had a great wish to make her happy, the happiest girl in the world. A very proper and almost fatherly feeling, he told himself. Even if they were of the same age, what of it? Men had to protect women. But why was he especially wishing to keep her here now? To talk to her? Yes, that was it. He wanted to talk to her, in a fatherly way, about life and serious things—all the things they had never spoken about before. It was true she had a father of her own, the Commander of the Scottish Archers. But who knew how good a father he was anyhow?

As she began for the third time to tell him she must be leaving, both the dogs barked together. The King's Finder took his fatherly eyes off the beautiful countess and looked across the lake. It was the figure of a man, over there, whose sudden approach had made the spaniels bark. Moreover, it was none other than his own esquire, Luke, waving and beckoning to him. Glad of a chance to delay her a little longer (and perhaps to invent further ways of keeping her out on her errand), Giles begged her to wait a moment while he went around the shore to speak with his esquire. And without giving her time to answer, he hurried away.

Luke had rather a queer look in his face, Giles thought, when he came up to him. Ordinarily these two young men were, of course, in the eyes of the court, master and servant, knight and esquire. And most of the time they had to act their different parts for the sake of appearances in the ceremonious life of the palace. But in real truth the pair were well-tried friends of almost lifelong standing. They shared each other's secrets and thoughts, and whenever they were alone together, and the world of princely pomp was not watching, they were equals and nothing more.

And that was why, when he came near to Luke this morning, Giles knew instantly there was something wrong. The esquire had a strange, ill-at-ease appearance about him, almost as though he had bad news for the King's Finder and didn't know quite how to set about breaking it.

"I—I am sorry," he began in a stammering kind of way, "very sorry to call you away like this when you were busy—er—with other matters. But I heard something a moment ago and I—I—er—hastened down to tell you of it. I thought perhaps it would be better that you heard it from me than from anyone else. You see—" Then he stopped and pulled at the head of a bullrush growing near by.

"Well!" said Giles. "Go on! What is it?"

"Maybe I'm wrong," Luke continued after a moment, "in making it my business to come and tell you. But—anyway—that's what I thought. The King's betrothal is to be announced this evening. He—he is going to marry the Countess Barbara—in a month from today."

A sharp, strange, almost unbearable feeling of hurt came into the heart of the young knight as he heard these words. There was no mistaking their meaning. Luke's news was clear and plainly spoken at the end, for all his hesitation to begin. There was no answer necessary, no need to repeat. The King was to marry Barbara.

Giles looked back across the lake. The slim, lovely girl was still standing at the farther shore, the lilies in her arms, waiting for him to return. But he was quite sure at once that he was not going to return. He would need time now before he could speak to her again—of just those ordinary things they always talked of, dogs and horses and the rest. Of a sudden the white figure at the water's edge grew dim before his eyes, as though a mist had risen from the lake between them.

And the King's Finder knew at last that he was himself in love.

For one mad second the idea came into his mind to run to her, to tell her everything and then escape with her into the mountains—anywhere, to get her away from the King. But what of her, Barbara, the new Queen to be? Why suppose she would want to come with him? She must know of this already. She must be willing. With her knowledge and consent the marriage had been arranged. And then, what of the King? The generous, kindly prince who had been so true a comrade, to whom he owed everything! What of the "friendship that does not betray"?

The mad moment passed. And Luke's keenly watching eyes saw the young knight's muscles tighten with a pitiful, determined courage as he gave up the rebellion in his heart. The esquire came quickly to Giles's side and, without speaking, gripped him firmly by the arm.

After a moment he heard his master speaking, but in a voice so low it could be barely heard: "Do you go around and join her, Luke. Make my excuses to her. I will return to the castle by this shore. Help her with the lilies to the Queen. If the King asks for me, I'll be at the stables. I've a notion to see Midnight the black mare."

CHAPTER FIVE

THE PRINCESS SOPHRONIA

Four weeks, all but a day, had passed. And the whole kingdom had taken on an air of great excitement, of happy expectation. Every town and village and hamlet was making ready for a holiday. For the subjects of the King, without waiting for any royal commands, had decided there should be national rejoicing at his marriage.

It looked, the older ones said, as though it would be an even greater celebration than when the young King was crowned. For then he had been little more than a lad. And a country never feels quite safe from revolution with a boy on the throne and a strong ambitious nobility thirsty for power. Nor had the people then known what manner of ruler this youngster would turn out to be. But after nine years of the Reign of Peace had rolled by, and the young King had shown his true greatness and generous nature, word had now been spread through the land that he was about to marry. And there was hardly one, even among the lowliest and most poor, who did not greet the news almost as though it were of a happy wedding in his own family.

This gladness was made greater still when it was learned that the King was marrying the lady of his heart, for love, and not a great princess to increase the power and wealth of the realm. Barbara was only a countess, a member of the lesser nobility, and had not even been seen by many, but it was said that her beauty was the rarest the land had ever known and her gracious kindness no less. Such a marriage of romance pleased the people far more than a great alliance to a neighboring kingdom—which, as often as not, meant nothing in the end but more wars and trouble. And they nodded their heads sagely as they made their villages gay for the festival, saying it was just like the young King to marry the girl he loved, the same as they would have done themselves.

But of course the fluttering excitement was highest of all at the castle itself. Here, as the great day came nearer, the happy bustle of preparation had grown and grown, till now, on the eve of the wedding, the great palace buzzed like a beehive under an August sun at noon.

Everyone, even the Queen Mother herself, had been untiringly busy. For while some hundreds of extra servants had been hired to do the actual work, it was necessary that they should be watched and guided every minute, and this was the duty of the old and trained retainers, the officers of the Royal Household, and the members of the King's own family. The Queen Mother devoted almost her whole attention to Barbara's new wardrobe. Gowns, gowns, and more gowns! By the score dressmakers, tailors, shoemakers, jewelers, and glovers were busy in her apartments at all hours. The well-beloved little old lady was determined that her son's wife should be the best-dressed queen that ever mounted the throne.

Never had so many guests been invited to the castle: dukes, bishops, princes, and even kings of foreign lands. A whole army of carpenters and workers had to be called in to put up new buildings in an unbelievably short time to provide quarters for all. And this, in order that everyone should have apartments worthy of his rank, with furniture and silken hangings and whatnot, required a lot of planning and overseeing.

The Chief of the Royal Cooks lost a lot of weight from his enormous figure getting in and storing away hundreds of wagonloads of good things to eat. He, too, was determined that his department should do its best, and better, at the great festival.

Then there were the games and entertainments to be looked to. The Master of the Horse, helped by Luke (who now showed great skill in riding and tilting), arranged a two days' program of tournament and joust, in which the foreign knights could try their lances against the nobles of the King. In this Giles's friend, the good Count Godfrey, also aided.

And Geoffrey (busy enough already raising wedding roses for a queen) was given a new task in the royal service. This was to search the country for players, acrobats, jugglers, and singers to entertain the King and his guests. The Gypsy, who knew the haunts of such troupes, soon gathered to the castle a whole host of show folk. These rehearsed merry plays and masques and dances on the green sward above the Lower Lake, now dotted with their tents.

Anne, also, was now at the court, a grown-up girl and Second Lady-in-waiting to the Queen Mother. It was about six weeks ago that she had first arrived. Giles was glad to see her and to get news of their parents and their native town. He also asked her about Agnes and was deeply disappointed to find his sister had not seen the Applewoman, nor heard of her, since he had left nearly nine years ago. Often, when he yet had the shell, he had listened for her voice in it. But with no success. He felt a great wish, almost a need, to see and talk with her at this time. Now he wondered sadly if she could be dead.

Anne soon settled down into the grand life of the Royal Household. But she could never quite seem to get used to her brother's important part in it. She twitted him with first hiding all the things he found for the King. This of course she only did, sisterlike, to tease

him. She had known well, even when they were both little, this great gift of his for finding which had now made him famous throughout the land. And the last few weeks she had seen him performing at his best.

For never before had Giles been kept so busy. With the palace packed and teeming from morn to night; with new servants and guests who didn't know their way about; with princes who brought with them dozens of grooms and horses and coaches filled with wedding presents, the poor Finder didn't know which way to turn. It was now persons as well as things he had to find. Often in the same hour he had not only to look for a lost piece of a guest's baggage but would have to go hunting a bishop or a prince who had gone astray. So great was the turmoil in the castle.

But Giles did not grumble at the extra work. He was indeed glad of it—to keep his mind from brooding on his own trouble. Ever since that day at the Lower Lake, he had carefully kept out of the Countess's way. He still could not trust himself to talk with her lest he speak of his love, and he was still desperately determined not to be untrue to the King, his friend.

He saw her but seldom, even at a distance, during those busy days of preparation. When he did, he noticed she seemed the least excited of all, still serious, still quiet. He supposed that it was merely that marriages interested her no more now than they had done when she was very young.

Not even to Luke had he ever spoken of the great longing in his heart, though the two talked of other matters freely enough. Nor had the esquire ever mentioned Barbara's name again to his master since he had brought him the news of her betrothal. It was as if that understanding friend, who had guessed the way the Finder's heart was yearning before he knew himself, felt that this was a matter for no more words.

But if Giles now saw very little of the Countess Barbara, he saw a great deal of the Princess Sophronia. In the last nine years that lady had not grown any younger—nor any better looking. The prince who was to have married her had changed his mind and gone elsewhere to seek another wealthy bride. So the flattering courtiers did not sing her praises anymore. Shortly after that Sophronia's hearing had grown worse, and she was now quite deaf.

At the announcement of the King's betrothal, she had appointed herself Mistress of Ceremonies and took general charge of all the preparations for the wedding. She had to do something to keep her self-importance. And a great nuisance she was to everybody. She pushed her nose in everywhere and kept changing this, or altering that, as soon as the others had completed some specially hard piece of work. And again, because she was the King's aunt, no one dared complain. But, oh, the things they said behind her back!

Her greatest joy and treasure was still the Whispering

Shell. This, after her promise to Giles, she never brought out or showed in public. But secretly in the privacy of her bedroom, she spent long hours with it, holding it, waiting for it to grow warm. And it often did, about that time, wax boiling hot. Which made the King's aunt very happy. For whenever anyone in the busy palace cried in despair, "Drat that ugly old fuss-box! I wish she'd mind her own business!" a gleam of joy would light up the face of the deaf Princess. And she would whisper to herself: "Ah, there they go! Still talking of my beauty. Patience, Royal Sophronia! Another prince will come."

CHAPTER SIX

The Eve of the Wedding

It was nearly midnight. At last the great work of getting ready for the wedding was all done. In spite of Princess Sophronia putting herself in charge, the Lord Chamberlain was now quietly going around to the heads of the different departments of the Royal Household to make sure that everything was complete and nothing overlooked. Of this all were heartily glad. For they were only awaiting his final inspection before going to bed. Tomorrow, the great day itself, would be a long one, they knew, and everybody wanted to get a good sleep before the gaieties began.

Giles was the last to go off duty and retire to his rooms. He could rest now, certain that nothing was lost or missing. But in spite of all the running around that he had done, he found he was not sleepy. Instead of getting into bed he threw open the window and sat down in a chair before it. The cool night air was soothing. But his mind would not stop working; it was full of worrisome ideas.

So, he thought, Barbara would be Queen tomorrow. No, today, for it was now past midnight. He would have to see more of her now, whether he wished it or no. After her coronation she would sit on a throne beside the King and be with him constantly. Would he himself be able to talk to Her Majesty like any of the other knights about the court? And the King? Would the close friendship between him and his Finder be the same now that he had a wife claiming his attention and sharing his plans? No, whichever way it was looked at, this marriage must make a big difference to them all. It would be better if he, Giles, went away now for a spell. For the present he feared he could not bear to see them together all the time. At the court it would not be possible to keep away from the King, as before he had been able to keep away from the Countess. Now they would be together, and he would have to be in attendance on them every day.

Yes—he got up and paced the floor as the idea grew in his mind—yes, that was the best plan. He needed a change. It was a good time, too, this, to ask permission to go on leave. For almost nine years he had been at his master's side with barely a break. The King would surely let him take a holiday. He would make a visit to his own town, his home. His parents, after all this time, would be glad to see him, their son, now grown into a man. And then Luke? Should he take him too?

He paused in his restless walk, wondering if Luke were still awake. The room had three doors to it, one that opened on the tower stairs, another that shut off Luke's bedroom, and a third leading through a short passage to the King's apartments. This, tonight, was ajar, and Giles saw the light of a candle showing dimly behind it. He knew that His Majesty had not yet come to bed, for he had seen him a little while since going toward the palace chapel with the Queen Mother. The grooms were probably asleep within, waiting for their master to retire. In the whole castle there was not a sound.

On tiptoe Giles had started toward Luke's room when he heard footsteps coming up the tower stairs. It sounded like several people, hurrying—but softly, without clatter. He watched the latch as it was lifted carefully from outside. Then the door silently flew open and two soldiers of the guard, with lanterns in their hands, stepped into the room.

They at once made way for those that followed: the King himself; the Queen Mother, weeping and clinging to his arm; and behind her, her Lady-in-waiting Anne.

The King's face looked like a ghost's. With a quick whispered command he dismissed the men-at-arms, bidding them leave their lanterns and to shut the door behind them. He motioned to Anne to close the entrance to his own rooms. The Queen Mother sank into a chair, sobbing softly.

The whole mysterious business puzzled Giles completely. But with the others present he asked no questions. He stood where they had found him, respectfully waiting for his master to speak first. For a little the King's face moved and twisted in a dreadful way, like someone choking for breath and words together.

"Giles," he gasped out at last, "I come to beg of you the greatest thing I have ever asked of any man—the most sacred task your service to me has ever been called upon to carry out. The Countess Barbara has disappeared, gone! And you must find her. You must, you *must!*"

He moved a step nearer and his clenched hands rose trembling in the air above his head. The Queen glanced nervously toward the door as his words grew louder.

"She's gone, Giles!" The King's voice broke down again to a choking whisper. "You must find her for me— Find her and bring her back!"

CHAPTER SEVEN

THE GREAT QUEST

And so Sir Giles Waggonwright, the King's Finder, set forth alone to seek the King's bride. His only companion was the horse he rode, Midnight. The famous black mare was older now but as clever, as gentle, as surefooted as ever, and her master could have asked for no better company to suit his mood today.

Not only was this task that lay ahead the greatest the King had ever given him, it was also the most difficult. He had nothing whatever to guide him in his search. All he knew was that the Countess Barbara had disappeared and left no trace behind her.

Before leaving the castle he had questioned the Queen Mother—also his own sister, who had been the last to see the Countess in the palace. Anne slept in the room next to Barbara's and had said good night to her when they both retired at ten o'clock. About half an hour later, she told her brother, a strong wind had begun to blow, and fearing the rattling windows might wake the Countess, she had gone into the next room. She found it empty, the bed not slept in, and no trace of Barbara anywhere.

When the Queen Mother had been told of this, she and the King had made a more thorough search to see if anything could be discovered that would help to solve the mystery. This was done with great secrecy, because the Queen was most anxious that the guests invited to the wedding should suspect nothing until the news could no longer be kept from them. Barbara's father, the Commander of the Scottish Archers, had been asked if he knew any cause or reason for so strange a business. But the poor man, almost crazed with grief, was just as puzzled as the King over his daughter's disappearance.

There were thus only five people in the palace who as yet knew, and they were of course terrified that some harm had come to the missing girl. All sorts of guesses were made as to what had become of her, but not one that brought any help or light or satisfaction. It was the King's opinion that she had been kidnapped—perhaps through a false message or some other means planned to lure her away beyond the castle walls; from there she could have been carried off swiftly, leaving no trace.

There was no one that the King could suspect directly of such a deed. But there were among his guests foreign kings and princes who had in former times been at war with his father. And it was possible that some one of them might have arranged the matter—helped by friends or retainers from outside—without appearing to have anything to do with it. To any bearing malice or envy against him, this would seem a sure way to bring ridicule or disgrace upon a great monarch: by taking his bride from his castle on the eve of the wedding.

This story or explanation was the only one the poor King could think of. Giles did not say whether he believed it or did not believe it. Anyhow, if it were true, it made secrecy doubly important. The only consolation he could offer to the King was that there were no signs of violence or a struggle left behind. This was at all events some comfort. Sometimes no news meant good news, he said.

After he had assured himself that no tracks were to be found beneath the windows of the Countess's room, he made certain that she could not be hidden anywhere in the castle—also that no horses were missing from the stables. Then he came to the King and his mother to bid them farewell.

So great was his faith in his own gift for finding—in his never-failing luck—that he told them he hoped to bring or send back news of the missing girl in two or three days at most. Meanwhile he begged them to take the greatest care that no word of Barbara's disappearance should leak out. Anne was to guard the Countess's room so that none should know that she was not still within the castle walls. He asked that Luke be taken into the secret and set to help his sister with her task. His search would be made easier so. There was no need, he said, that the wedding guests should be sent away for the present, but word ought to be given out that the marriage had had to be put off for a few days—to await the arrival of an important personage whose presence at the ceremony was necessary. Then, when the King had wished him good fortune, and the Queen Mother had given him her blessing, he had ridden forth alone.

He had appeared sure and confident enough when he was still with them, hoping to cheer their sad hearts. But after he was well away from the castle, he was bound to admit that he had very little to build his hopes on. And the more he thought of his task, the harder it seemed. In all the difficult searches he had made so far, he had begun by carefully thinking out a plan of action. Yet here for the first time, with the whole world for a hunting ground, he could scarcely think of any worthy of the name.

The best he could do, he decided, was to work over the country in circles, keeping the castle as a center. It was barely twelve hours since Barbara had left. She could not therefore at most be farther off than a fast horse could carry her in that time. So it was his hope that in crossing all the roads that led away from the palace, he might hear word or by some other good turn of fortune find which one it was she had traveled by.

But even if he was somewhat downcast about the

success of his search, he had also a curious feeling of gladness as he rose in his stirrups to Midnight's fast and steady forward-swinging trot. He was glad that Barbara had not been made Queen this morning. He was glad that she was still unmarried. Then instantly remembering the King's grief, he was ashamed of such thoughts. Nevertheless that odd spark of happy thrill would come tingling back through his blood once in a while. Till at length he gritted his teeth as he urged his horse into a better speed. He told himself that now, if ever, he must be on guard against his own feelings. And if he could not entirely rid his heart of such disloyal ideas, he must force them to help him toward a higher unselfishness in the service of his King and friend.

He had intended not to break the first stage of his journey till he had gained a point some twenty miles at least from the capital. Then he would begin his circling search. At that distance fewer people would know him by sight. In and around the castle it would be already noted that Sir Giles Waggonwright had set out upon a journey. But so long as he was careful, no one need learn for the present what errand it was that took him forth.

By nightfall he had reached a village. Here he made his first halt. It was at the crossing of several roads, one of them quite an important highway for traffic, such as it was in those times. This place, Giles felt, would be a good one from which to start his work. In questioning the country folk he could not of course speak of the

Countess Barbara by name, nor even ask directly if they had seen a young woman of her description. He had to get information in a roundabout sort of way by chatting with the villagers on all sorts of general country gossip, hoping that some word would be let fall that would start him on the right track.

Remembering that the girl, on their trips into the country with the King and Luke, had always been kind to the poor and unfortunate, he kept an eye open for any beggars whom he could engage in conversation. Also her liking for horses and dogs led him to visit all the stables he passed. Asking after good horses to hire gave him an excuse to speak with grooms and ostlers who might have seen her. He took Midnight into every blacksmith's shop he saw to have her hooves looked at or to get her bit and trappings shined up. At some places he didn't do any talking at all himself but just stood around listening to the exchange of gossip among the common people. In those times most news was carried by word of mouth. And now and then, knowing that the appearance of a knight might make the yokels too respectful and untalkative, he would pretend to fall asleep from weariness in taverns or on public benches. He hoped he might more easily so catch something helpful to his search.

But his stay in the first village brought him nothing, and the following morning, early, he moved on to the westward.

He knew the country well, every inch of it. The need

to hurry now urged and worried him. And he planned this second day to visit at least five villages, not very far apart, that lay along the bank of one of the more important rivers flowing down from the mountains to the sea. This ought to bring him half of the way around his circle about the capital. Surely, he thought, somewhere on that distance a trace or clue might lead him to the missing girl. So, touching the mare's flanks lightly with his riding whip, he set out hopefully.

Hopefully? (His horse came to a sudden standstill without command.) Again Giles had that queer sense of being somehow almost glad that he had not yet succeeded, that his beloved Barbara was still unmarried and uncrowned. It was whispering now like some doughty little demon, away down in the heart of him—him, the great King's Finder who had never failed upon a quest! . . .

A cock crowed harshly from a farm nearby.

Then, impatient, Midnight shook her handsome head and pawed the gravel.

Sir Giles Waggonwright rode on.

CHAPTER EIGHT

Wonder World

The sea glimmered in a rosy twilight. It was the evening of the second day of search. Far off, at the edge of the quiet ocean, the sails of little ships, like bits of black cardboard, moved very slowly along the skyline. Drawn up on the beach nearer at hand were more boats, with fishermen spreading out their nets and coiling ropes. Around them white gulls soared, faintly squealing. A solitary man stood on the cliffs above, looking down at it all. From his dress he would have been taken for a pilgrim. For he wore a long cloak of coarse cloth, had sandals on his feet, carried a staff cut from the hedges, and showed all the appearance of those who travel hard journeys afoot to visit shrines and far-off places of worship. Not even a friend, unless he looked closely under the wide hat shading the man's face, would have known that it was Giles.

There was a worried weariness in his eyes. The five

villages he had come through since daybreak had given him nothing of hope, not a trace of her whom he sought, not a hint of which direction to run his search in. Thinking that he might draw less attention to himself and be better able to ask questions, he had changed from his ordinary clothes to those of a poor wanderer begging his way. And so he had come at length to the sea. Now he was asking himself as he gazed down upon it, could Barbara have gone beyond, over the wide waters into foreign lands? This small fishing port below was the nearest harbor to the capital. He had questioned the seamen on the sands. But they could tell him nothing. Nevertheless without their knowledge she might have been carried away on any of the vessels sailing down the river at night. Supposing she had, what chance was left for him of overtaking her?

If only he had not been in such a hurry with his rash promises! "In two or three days," he had told the King. What a mad boast! Here was the last of the second day fading from his sight, and he had nothing to show for his work but a great weariness of body and puzzlement of mind.

Standing up there alone at the cliff's edge, he breathed the live sea air deep into his tired body. Another day gone. In spite of the thousand questions that turned and jumbled in his mind, he could not help being thrilled by the glory of such an evening. He felt at once weakly small and humbly great. From here his eyes could sweep the world: gray sea below; darkening land behind; the sky a great violet ceiling overhead with rags of pink-edged clouds; the single spark of a lone star, steady glowing, where the sun had sunk . . . Barbara! Where was she now? What was she thinking of? Why had she gone?

Could not some wizard, some magic wish giver, come to his aid, wave a wand to lift her out of this silent world and place her at his side, here on the cliff top? Night putting her arms around the sea. No helping wizard. Just the earth going to bed the same as it had done for a million years, prosy, practical, and prompt. Were no more wonders worked since sprites and fairies left the haunts of man? Yet it was magic, too, this—so Geoffrey would have said—the sun sinking in the sea at dusk and rising on the land at dawn. And so it looked in truth. Gorgeous colors, violet, rose, and silver-gray, moving, changing, mingling aswirl. The day of mystery, wonder stuff, and witchcraft, of elves and goblins, jinns and mermaids, fading into quiet dark like the peaceful sleepy ending of enchanted dreams.

Was it the Twilight of Magic? Perhaps. But only today's. Magic could never die while the sun had the power to rise again and man had the wish to seek.

Giles pulled his rough cloak more closely about his shoulders. If tomorrow's work should bring no more than today's, he asked himself, what then? He would have failed. A great finder he, failing his master in his worst need!

And had he really tried his hardest? His conscience

nagged at him unmercifully. That little voice of gladness had so often whispered. Could it be said that the only time he failed was when the King sent him seeking his own great love?

No, no, no! That should not be. He would not be beaten. She must be found. Soon he would run into his finder's luck again if he only kept on. And what was he wasting time for here, standing and thinking and looking at sunsets, when there was so much need for haste? A day, a few hours only, and he would have to send word to the castle: yes or no.

He took up his staff, which had fallen to the ground. But before turning away from the brink of the cliff, he gave a last glance at the sea. It was much darker now and his eyes could no longer make out the sails of the tiny craft creeping along the edge of the world. The ocean would always be linked in his mind with Agnes, the roar of surf, the Whispering Shell. Oh, if he only had it now! In the time of two days Barbara would surely have spoken of him, or if she had been kidnapped, then the men who held her would. For their greatest fear must be of him, the King's Finder.

He hurried away across the turf toward the road by which he had come.

Yes, the shell would have been a great help. Yet how could he have taken it? He had promised and given it to the Princess Sophronia. It was no longer his. And no power would have made her give it up willingly. It was a strange thing, that shell. From long experience of it he had grown to look on its queer powers as something quite everyday and ordinary—like a window in your house where you went to listen for the voices of returning children or the barking of your dog. Yet it *was* strange—magic or science, mystery or common sense, who would ever find out? What a pity the King had cast it from him that night! And yet perhaps not. It could bring evil as well as aid. That was certain.

Well, he must do without it now and get on with his business.

The road he was seeking was a small cart track which led up to these cliffs from the village he had last halted at. In that village he had left Midnight and the clothes he had worn when he had ridden away from the castle. He hoped, as he peered about him in the half dark, that the keeper of the inn who had stabled his horse would also have prepared a good supper for himself. He was terribly hungry.

His foot touched something hard in the turf. It was the road. Looking ahead, he could now see lights.

The pilgrim gripped his staff and set off for the village at a quick walk.

CHAPTER NINE

THE SADDLEBAG

The first thing Giles did on reaching the village inn was to go and see how his mare was faring. In the stable yard he noticed another horse, saddled and bridled, standing near the well. It was breathing hard, its hide damp with sweat. Another guest had come while he was out. The Finder was of course very interested just now in arrivals of any kind. From the open door of the stable where he had left Midnight, he heard the sound of talking. He paused a moment to listen before going in.

The voices were two. One Giles recognized immediately as the innkeeper's. The other, for the moment, he was not so sure of, though it sounded somehow like one he ought to know well. Certainly the newcomer, whoever he was, had been asking about the black mare, for the host of the inn was now telling him at what hour she had come, what her rider had looked like, and a great deal more. Then the other asked some further questions. And this time Giles knew the voice beyond all doubt. It was Luke's.

At once he was about to rush in and welcome his old friend. But on second thought he changed his mind and drew back from the door. Naturally the esquire would not have told the host why either of them had come to his inn. And for other reasons, too, it would be better if they had their first meeting alone. Therefore he walked quietly back across the yard, entered the house, and went upstairs to his room. Here, he was sure, Luke would presently come seeking him. For with Midnight in the stable the esquire must know that his master would soon return. Meanwhile, after changing his clothes, Giles rinsed his hands and face in a copper wash basin that stood on the table.

The evening was warm, and while he freshened himself up, he left the dormer window open. Through it he could see right across the river to the far shore. Lights twinkled from a group of cottages clustered at the water's edge. Behind them the black shadow of a hill rose against the clear night sky, topped by a long straggling building of very beautiful architecture. This was lit up, too, though dimly. But even at that distance one could tell that the north end of it was a chapel. For the rich colors of a fine stained-glass window were brought out clearly by the candlelight behind.

He had just finished drying his face when a knock sounded on the door.

"Come in!"

Luke entered with a candle in his hand and a saddle-bag under his arm. He closed the door behind him before any word was spoken.

"It is more than good to see you," said Giles. "You've been up to my tricks: traced me by the mare, eh? Well, a horse is always easier to track than a man. Throw the bag on the floor and sit down. But how did you know what road I had taken?"

"I watched from the castle tower," said Luke. "Before you were out of sight, I guessed you were making for the Harbour Turnpike—though which direction you'd go in when you struck it, I could not tell, of course. However, a few questions at the wayside inns soon put me on your trail—and once found, it was not hard to stick to. Is there any—er—any news?"

"Of the Countess? No," said Giles. "I have never been so completely puzzled in my life. But you must have more news than I. First, why did you come after me?"

Giles seated himself on the bed while Luke talked.

"Well, for one thing, both the King and the Queen Mother were terribly anxious for word of you. Almost ever since you left, His Majesty has been watching from the tower windows for messengers. For another thing, I guessed you would be wanting more clothes. You had taken barely anything but what you stood up in. And then besides, naturally, I wanted to come too. Anne didn't really need my help: You might. So I asked His Majesty if he would let me go after you with a second tunic and some fresh linen. He seemed very pleased at the idea and gave me leave at once."

"Humph!" Giles muttered. "It was thoughtful of you—about the clothes, I mean. But I had asked you to stay with Anne. Was there no other reason for your leaving the castle?"

"Of course there was," Luke added with an odd kind of sheepish look. "I would not else have gone against your orders, you may be sure. But something—two things—happened after you went away. I did not speak to the King of them. And they may not, even to you, seem of any importance. Just the same, I thought you might want to know of them. The Whispering Shell—"

Giles sprang to his feet.

"It's lost," said Luke. "Just disappeared. The Princess Sophronia came to me yesterday in a terrible state. Said it had been stolen from her room. Anne and I hunted everywhere for it. We had hard work to keep the old lady from rushing all over the palace claiming she had been robbed. Then, when we couldn't find it, she told me she was certain you had taken it with you, since you alone had keys to all the palace doors. She wanted to have me put under arrest for even daring to argue with her. But at last Anne got her calm enough to answer a few questions. And we soon found out that she had had the shell in her own hands, once at least, *since* you had left. So she had to admit that you couldn't have taken it. However, I told her I'd try to get the King's permission to come after you and would ask you to look for it.

And it was only then that she quieted down enough so Anne and I dared leave her."

"What time was it yesterday that she came to you?" Giles asked.

"About noon, I should say."

The King's Finder walked thoughtfully across the room. He halted at the open casement, looking out over the river.

"Well," he asked presently, "what was the other thing that happened?"

"You remember the two black spaniels the Countess owned," asked Luke, "Maggie and Mollie?"

"Yes. Of course I do."

"Well, one of them appears to have turned into a large black cat," Luke announced quite solemnly.

Sharply Giles turned his head.

"Are you trying to joke, Luke?" he snapped out angrily. "Whoever heard of such nonsense?"

"I know that's what it sounds like," said the esquire. "But if you had seen what I have, you'd understand why I put it that way. The Countess always kept the two dogs in her room, you remember. After Anne and I had pacified the old Princess, we went back there. And one of the spaniels was missing—Mollie. In its place, playing with Maggie in the most friendly fashion, was a large black cat. But the most peculiar part was that the cat used all the same tricks—you know, ways of pouncing and attacking in fun—that Mollie used."

"Did it make any sounds?" asked Giles.

"Not catlike sounds at all," said Luke. "But he growled like a dog when he got knocked down in the sham fighting, exactly the way that Mollie used to growl. You would have to see him to understand it. He was like a dog in every way he acted, but he was still a cat to look at. Anne said she could nearly believe it *was* Mollie, dressed up in a cat's skin. And Maggie's behavior was peculiar too. You'd think she'd want to fight with a cat instead of playing with him, just from natural dog's instinct—let alone from jealousy at his coming into her mistress's home—you know how pets are that way. But not at all. She treated the cat as though he were the oldest friend she had, let him sleep in the same basket with her and everything. Didn't seem to miss Mollie, either. It almost looked as though the cat had come specially to take Mollie's place and keep the other dog from grieving over the loss of her playmate. Anne is positive that he is one of Agnes's cats. Though I don't see any particular reason for thinking that."

"Except that he never cries, meows, or makes what you called catlike sounds, eh?" muttered Giles. "Have you or Anne had any news of Agnes?"

"No," said Luke. "It is hardly likely that we would, is it? Nine years now since we saw or heard of her."

"You haven't spoken of the cat to anyone at the palace?"

"No. The beast of his own accord keeps out of everyone's way. And Anne thought it best not to talk about it—with the wedding so near and all. Black cats are supposed to bring bad luck when they cross your path."

"I know." Giles nodded. "People still believe in superstitions like that, rubbish that has no rhyme or reason or sense whatever. While anything unusual that Agnes might do, like curing your leg, they'd call incantation, sorcery, sinful Devil dealing, and whatnot. 'Shragga the Witch!' Bah!"

"Poor Agnes!" murmured Luke. "I wonder what corner of the world she's hiding her old head in now."

"Who can tell?" Giles sighed. "And yet you know, sometimes—lately—I've had a sort of feeling—I can't explain it. A feeling that she's not far off, that that powerful mind of hers is around us, near, now, in touch almost with my own. I haven't felt so in a long, long time, not since Anne and I stayed that night at the Haunted Inn and met all those strange dreamfolk—who talked to us but didn't seem quite real. . . . I don't know. Perhaps it's all nonsense. Maybe it's just that I'm mortal tired. Yet that matter of the shell's disappearing is queer enough. Hah! A busy time for the King's Finder! Everything's disappearing. I suppose the castle itself will be the next. But as for the dog, that does not seem hard to explain. The Countess took the spaniel with her for company, most likely. I wish I had known that before I left. It might have helped me in the search. But I was in such a hurry to catch up with her, I couldn't spare much time. How were things faring at the palace when you left?"

"Oh, well enough, considering all. No suspicion of

the Countess's going seems to have leaked out—though how much longer that can be kept up I do not know. We have been most careful, keeping the wedding guests busy with games, races, shows, dances, and whatnot. The Queen Mother has been wonderful, hiding her worry behind a smiling face and taking part in everything. The Count Godfrey too."

"And the King?" asked Giles.

Luke frowned uneasily at the floor. "He has not seemed so well. Tries hard to act a good host's part to all his guests. But looks pale, with his thoughts a hundred miles away. He eats hardly at all. Most of the daylight hours, as I said, he spends up in the tower watching the road below."

Giles turned back to the open window and for a moment said nothing more. Over the dark hill beyond the river, a wisp of a slanting moon could now be seen. Its pale path shimmered dimly in the quiet water below. Luke crossed the room, put his hand upon his master's shoulder, and looked out. A ferryboat with long sweeping oars crept out from the shadow of the farther shore and slid silently toward them. Suddenly the noise of bells broke the hush with a distant silvery voice.

"What does that mean?" asked Luke, gazing up at the hill.

"Chapel bells," said Giles. "Vespers. That's the Convent of Saint Bridget up there, the long building at the top of the ridge."

"You do know this country, don't you?" said Luke.

"I suppose you'd be bound to, after nine years at your work. Convent of Saint Bridget, eh? Looks like a big place. . . . Listen, Giles: how about some supper? You must be hungry—and I know I am. Let me go down and rout out that lazy old host of ours. And I must see if he has put my horse to bed yet. I'll not be long."

He started toward the door.

"Oh, and you won't forget the saddlebag," he added. "You'll find a fresh shirt in it, if you've a mind to rid yourself of some of the road dust. I'll give you a call as soon as the food is ready."

CHAPTER TEN

THE POCKET OF THE TUNIC

For a moment longer Giles remained looking out at the ferryboat before he closed the window part way and turned to the saddlebag. He opened it without much interest and spread its contents on the bed.

Besides the newly laundered linen there was a tunic, some hose, a pair of gloves, and other things. He could hear Luke below shouting for the host, then the clatter of footsteps and his cheerful whistle as he crossed the stable yard to look to his horse.

The idea of a clean shirt after so much hard travel seemed very welcome to Giles. In less than a minute he had changed. He was about to get into his old jacket when he noticed it was muddy on one sleeve. He took up the tunic from the bed. It was a newer and a lighter one than that which he had worn for the last two days. He put it on and threw the old one over a chair. Then he lay back on the bed to wait for Luke's call to supper.

It seemed as though the esquire had not found everything to his liking in his horse's stall. For presently his
voice could again be heard calling impatiently for the
innkeeper.

Waiting and weary, Giles must have dozed off into a
short sleep. Because suddenly he sat up, wondering
where he was. He rubbed his eyes. He was more certain
of being sharply aroused than he was of having fallen
asleep. He was sure, too, that he had been often brought
to his senses by the same thing before, though as yet
his drowsy mind could not give a name to it.

Then his hand flew to his side. Yes—hot! Something
was burning in the pocket of his new tunic. Frantically
he pulled it out. He had been awakened by the Whispering Shell!

Without stopping to wonder how or when it had come
there, he clapped it to his ear while it was warm. Words,
clear and sharp, as though the speaker were beside him!
His very heart seemed to stand still to help him listen
with all the attention of his soul. For it was the voice of
Barbara that he heard.

"The King's Finder. He is very clever, very skillful.
But I do not believe he can find us here. No, not now.
For this is the end of the journey."

Who could it be that she was speaking to? thought
Giles. . . . The voice went on gently, sadly: "How clear
the water was! And such a beautiful day! Do you remember the wide green sward sweeping up to the castle hill,

the oak trees clumped about the slope, the soft warm air, the glorious scent of the wet lilies? No? But you cannot have forgotten *him*, the young man, tall and strong, the King's Finder, who threw sticks into the lake for you to bring ashore?"

There came a high, sharp bark.

Mollie!

It was to her dog the Countess Barbara was speaking. Then the jingling of a silver collar. The spaniel was scratching her ear, humbly thoughtful, no doubt, of that great battle in the lake where she had lost the swimming championship to Maggie. A pause of silence followed. And Giles found his hand trembling like a leaf as the shell cooled slowly. Was the beloved voice going to say no more? What had she meant by "the end of the journey"? Was he not to learn after all where that journey ended, where she was now? Where, where, *where?*

But suddenly the heat glowed up again within his palm. And the words ran on: "Sir Giles Waggonwright, the truest man in the royal service. I hope this does not injure him at the court: failing but once, after succeeding so faithfully and long. They'll all be wondering what has befallen me—thinking maybe I am dead. My poor father, the good Queen Mother, and the King. It is wrong of me to keep them thus in ignorance. Yet it couldn't be helped. And oh, my Mollie dear, I want so to sit out here on the grass a while longer, before we go in. They will all learn soon enough where we are, even if the Finder could not trace us. It will not matter now, a short while still in freedom, under the stars and the little wide-roaming moon."

Something that might have been a sob broke into the words. But almost instantly, growing brave and firm again, the voice went on: "Yes, soon we'll go in. You, too, my Mollie. I think they'll let me bring you with me. I'll ask the Lady Abbess. She was a friend of my mother's years ago. You shall be a nun too—though you'll have to be less frisky, even if you don't wear the veil and gown. Yet we must not delay too long lest Sir Giles overtake us after all. A few minutes more and we'll ring the bell at the big gate there. . . . We'll go in. . . . Then we'll be Sisters, Sisters of Saint Bridget."

Giles sprang off the bed. Thrusting the shell, still warm, into his pocket, he leapt across the room and pulled the door open.

"Host!" he yelled. "Hulloa, below there! Host!"

"Coming, sir, coming," called a voice in the distance. In another moment the innkeeper's face appeared, with a candle held beside it, peering openmouthed from the foot of the staircase.

"Saddle the black mare," Giles shouted. "Quick! Don't stand there gaping. Bring Midnight to the door. Run, I tell you, *run!*"

CHAPTER ELEVEN

THE EBB TIDE

Luke had just come in from the stables. It was while he was still in the little dining room, looking over the supper laid out there, that he heard Giles shout. He immediately came into the hall to see if he could be of any help. There he was bumped into, first by the innkeeper dashing for the yard, and then by Giles himself leaping down the stairs two steps at a time. His master grabbed him by the arm and poured words into his ear as though his very life depended on their speed.

"Get yourself a fresh horse, Luke, and ride for the castle at once. You'll have to travel all night. Change mounts a dozen times if need be. Beg, borrow, or take them—I'll look after that later. Don't go around by the Harbour Turnpike. Take the shortcut across the moors. You ought to reach the palace by daybreak, or soon after. Tell the King, Barbara is safe and unharmed. There was no kidnapping. That's all I know now. But you can promise him that if everything goes as I hope, I'll bring her back before sunset tomorrow. Where's that fool of an innkeeper? Why doesn't he hurry? Here's some money. You pay the reckoning here. And tell me, did you put anything in the pocket of this tunic when you packed it?" (Luke shook his head.) "No, of course not. Well, never mind that now. There isn't a second to lose. Where *is* that man? Ah, I hear Midnight now. He's bringing her to the front door here. Good-bye, Luke. May good luck travel with us both!"

The door opened and slammed. The rest was a clatter of horse's hooves galloping down the road.

While the dazed Luke tried to pull his wits together, his speeding master was thinking of that ferryboat. Would it be this side or the other side of the river?

Barbara so near! Who would have guessed it? Up there at the convent gate. And he wondering just a little while ago if she had crossed the seas! Finder's luck!

In five minutes he had reached the landing. No boat in sight. He would not wait for it. It was a slow craft anyhow. He gauged the distance across the river with his eye. Yes, Midnight had swum farther than that in her day. Now, at the light touch of his spur, she leapt clean from the wharf's edge into the dark water. Then with long steady strokes she churned her way out into the stream.

Giles, as he had often done before, slipped out of the saddle. This to free her of his weight. And with his right hand twined in her flowing mane, he half swam, and was half towed, beside her. He peered ahead, upward at the lights of the convent chapel. The distance looked greater from here than it had from the boat landing.

Presently, nearly in mid-river, a current was felt. It grew in strength with almost overpowering suddenness. Both beast and man were being borne downstream at a terrifying speed. The thought of the sea, so close, flashed into Giles's mind. What if they should be swept clear out into the ocean? The tide was certainly at full ebb.

He thought of letting Midnight go, free to gain the shore of her own accord without the drag of his body. A good swimmer himself, he could likely reach the shore alone. But he decided that once separated, they might have difficulty finding each other again in the darkness on the land. It was a risk and at best would mean a loss of precious time.

No, he would cling on, and together they must do their best. He could hear her breathing hard as she changed direction a little, to head more upstream and make the crossing aslant. For Midnight, too, knew the danger of that ebb tide with the smell of the sea so near. Close by her neck, he gasped endearing words up into her ear to cheer her on. And in answer her mighty heels kicked at the evil, dragging current with still greater strength.

Soon, wriggling his arms out of the sleeves, he pulled

off his tunic and stuffed it into one of the saddlebags. He could swim better so, he hoped, and give the mare more help. But it did not seem to make much difference. His heavy spurred riding boots were his greatest hindrance. He should have thought to take them off before he leapt his horse into the stream. The current was getting stronger and the mare's breath shorter. The lights in the convent chapel seemed to be going farther away, inland, instead of coming nearer. From this point he could now see the dark gray horizon line of the sea, stretching across the river mouth.

Miserably he was blaming himself for his rash stupidity in not waiting for the ferry when suddenly Midnight's hooves ground into something hard. Her great shoulders climbed, looming up into the air above him, and in the same second his own feet touched bottom. They had reached a shoal.

The shore was still a long way off. Near, around them, nothing but darkness and water. It seemed it was a gravel bar they must be standing on, risen with happy unexpectedness from out of the river's gloomy heart to hold them up. Over this hidden island, though, the tide was rushing out with a force that threatened to knock them down again any moment. Wading, staggering, floundering waist deep, Giles felt and hunted till he found a shallower spot where they might rest and get their breath. Here the stream raced even faster still but not deep enough to be dangerous. Midnight shook the water from her flanks with a sighing, thankful snort. While Giles, too breathless to speak, too weary to stand alone, leaned upon her withers.

So for a while they stood, horse and man, under the stars out there, like ghostly statues in a flat and empty world. No sound broke the peace of their grateful rest but the gurgling of the river around their ankles and their own breath pumping in and out.

Giles was the first to move. Still dead weary, he was itching to hurry on. The very idea of food was long since forgotten. But, at that, he had had an easier fight than Midnight. The mare's neck was still stretched downward and forward in that hangdog fashion that shows a horse badly spent. There was no telling whether there would be more swimming ahead, or if the shore could be reached by wading. In spite of the pressing need for haste, he dared not, and would not, risk ruining her wind. She must have some minutes at least.

Meanwhile, what of Barbara? Had she gone into the convent by now? His work was difficult enough already without added difficulties with the nuns. He clenched his hands in desperate powerless impatience. What would he do? What *could* be done besides wait!

But the shell! Maybe he might learn something more from that quarter.

In an instant he had felt along his horse's back and was tugging at the wet tunic, trying to get it out of the saddlebag. How stubbornly it stuck! Then, as so often happens, it came flying out of a sudden, like a crumpled flag.

There was a flash—and a splash. In the tussle the shell had fallen from the tunic pocket into the rushing stream. Giles leapt for it, grabbing and snatching on his knees in the wet gloom. But the pale starlight had given him only one glimpse: when it first struck the water, turned over like a fish—green above and white below— then sped away, in the rolling, tumbling ebb tide, downstream.

For a moment, still on his hands and knees in the water, he gazed after it wide-eyed and dazed—while the truth slowly took shape in his mind. The Whispering Shell was gone—and with it the secret of its power— forever! Who now would ever learn whether it were magical or no? Underneath that flat, wet darkness it was rolling along the gravel floor of the river, rolling back to the home from which it came, the sea!

Giles lifted his dripping body upright. "Well," he muttered, "for good or bad, that means its work is done."

A bell tinkled softly from the convent on the hill. Barbara, perhaps, ringing to be let in.

He looked again at Midnight. Dared he push on yet? Brave Midnight! She seemed somewhat less droopy, and her breathing calmer. A light breeze came whispering down the river, very chilly to wet skins. Suddenly the mare raised her head and pawed the water as though she would be glad to be out of this.

Leading her on a long rein, Giles set off toward the shore. Going ahead very, very carefully, he felt out every yard of the way with his feet, on guard for hidden holes or sudden drops. And though the depths kept changing—sometimes breast high, sometimes no more than a few inches—he finally crossed the whole distance to the land without mishap.

Directly he was clear of the mud and reeds along the water's edge, he swung himself into the saddle and patted Midnight on the neck.

"Now, old friend," he whispered, gathering the reins in his hands, "you've shown a brave spirit. But your trickiest work lies still ahead. We've got to get to the top of that hill, to the main gate of the convent, as fast as it can possibly be done. And it's very little help that I can give you. Get to it now and warm yourself up."

The mare, as though she understood his words and knew the great importance of her help, never showed her surefooted cleverness better than she did that night. Her rider barely once drew the bit against her mouth. In a moment, as if by magic, she had found a trail. It might have been an old disused towpath or something of the kind. And while it had plenty of breaks and washouts along it, it led in the right direction, inland. Midnight turned her back to the sea and followed it. There were stretches where trees and high alders, overhanging the way, shut out even the poor light of the stars and waning moon. But not even the pitch-dark seemed to hinder her greatly. She covered the ground in short, quick rushes. Every once in a while she would pull up sharp, sniffing, snorting, and pawing—as fhough by some unknown sense she knew that here a bad place lay, some hidden danger or a bend in the trail. Then in a moment, full of comfortable confidence, she would rattle along again—over gravel, turf, or rock—a man could only tell the nature of the going by the sound.

Giles had often said that his beloved mare could see in the dark. Certainly anyone who had watched her then must have admitted that for this sort of work she had no equal. The King never gave a finer gift than this queen among horses—or named one better—Midnight.

CHAPTER TWELVE

THE ABBESS OF SAINT BRIDGET'S

The towpath and the sparsely wooded river land had now been left behind. On the open windswept slope of the hill, horse and rider stood out against the deep night-blue sky. The road leading up to the convent was well made and had not been hard to find. But it had soon become so steep in places that the impatient Giles had from time to time been forced to bring the pace down to a walk.

As he drew nearer to the hilltop, his mind grew more and more uneasy and his heart seemed to be beating in a silly, fluttery sort of way. Not only was he feverishly worried about his success (many slips and mischances were yet possible, he knew), but the thought of seeing Barbara again, of taking her back to the palace, disquieted and upset him terribly. In her talk with Mollie he had thought he heard sounds of weeping. What would be her mood when he met her? He would have to be on his guard against his own feelings, against woman's tears, against anything and everything.

No, this was something that had to be done and done quickly. The fewer words he used over it the better. His own wishes and opinions must be downed and silenced. He would come to her as nothing more than one of His Majesty's servants with orders to carry out.

But what if she should refuse to go back with him?

Well, he would have to be stern—that's all—stony-hearted and stern. No weakness now.

The poor man's fear that, with the end of the quest so near at hand, his love for this beautiful girl might interfere with his duty to the King was very real. So that he was not only all prepared to be stern and business-like, but he actually had his teeth set with determination when at last he did see her.

This was exactly where he had expected. At the very top of the hill, he had found a flat lawn, very wide and smooth, stretching the whole way along the front of the convent buildings. He could not yet see where the main gate was. But he heard Mollie bark in the distance. By following this sound he soon came upon a beautiful archway in a high stone wall, curving over a wooden door. Nearby he saw a white figure seated on the grass holding a growling black spaniel by the collar. His quick-beating heart gave one enormous thump and then raced on again faster than ever. So, she had not yet gone in!

He would no doubt have felt grateful for his famous luck if he had not been so taken up with being stiff and stern. He even tried to avoid looking at her as he swung down from his saddle and came a step or two nearer. At this distance Mollie recognized him, and breaking out of her mistress's grasp, she rushed bounding around his knees, wagging, and wriggling with joy.

The sound of singing came faintly from the chapel. Midnight stretched down her head and cropped the grass.

"Countess—"

He stopped with a question in his voice. He did not quite know why. Instantly the white figure leapt up and ran to him.

"Giles! How did you know I—"

"Madam," he broke in (the harshness in his voice silenced her), "the King has sent me to you."

She came a step nearer still, hesitatingly. Even in that dim light Giles could see the glorious beauty of her face puzzling over this awkward greeting, this unfriendly manner of his. He half turned his head and, looking away toward the distant sea, spoke on quickly.

"His Majesty wishes you to return to the castle at once."

Over his shoulder he heard her answer, low yet clear.

"But I do not wish to come."

Giles's jaw set a little firmer still.

"Your Ladyship must please understand. My orders were to find you and *bring* you back."

"Bring me back!" Her voice rose slightly, both pride and annoyance in its tone. "Am I then no more than an old coat or something, that the King's Finder has been sent out to fetch me in? I have journeyed here to enter the nunnery of Saint Bridget. I will not come with you."

Her anger was what saved him. He was still fighting the great longing in his heart, a longing now that cried out to him to clutch her in his arms, to tell her how madly happy he was to see her again, to find her safe and well. And if she had shown tears or begged him to take her side in this matter, he might easily have given way. Then, in spite of all determinations, his errand of trust would likely have come to failure at the last. But her wrathful rebellion against the orders of the King helped him play his part of sternness and duty. Showing an anger of his own to cover other feelings, he suddenly turned and looked her full in the eye.

"Very well, my lady. If you would put it so, you must not blame me for the consequences. You force me to place you under arrest."

For one moment she stared back at him defiantly. Then she ran swiftly to the convent gate and pulled at something that hung beside the door. Instantly a bell clanged out into the stillness of the night. Its ringing dwindled slowly, then came to rest in silence.

"Your Ladyship has saved me the trouble," said Giles. "I was about to do that myself."

His surprising words seemed to change her mood a little.

"But you don't understand," she cried. "You know nothing of my reasons for—"

Quickly he interrupted her.

"It is not my business to learn your reasons. Those you can tell to the King. My orders were only to find you and bring you back."

From within the courtyard behind the wall, they heard hurrying footsteps—then the rattle of bolts. The heavy gate swung slowly inward. In the opening stood a Sister, peering out at them with a lantern in her hand. Giles immediately stepped forward.

"May I speak with the Mother Abbess?" he asked.

"She is in the chapel now, sir, at vespers," the nun answered. "If you will wait till the service is over, I will ask her."

"I am sorry, but waiting is impossible," said Giles. "Pray take her my regrets for this disturbance and say the reason for my coming here is most urgent."

The Sister hurried away.

While she was gone, Giles moved back and pretended to busy himself with the trappings of his horse. He felt that the less talk he had with Barbara from now on the better. But presently she came to his side.

"What do you want the Abbess for?" she asked. "What do you mean to do with me?"

"Nothing very terrible," he answered, tugging at a strap. "But I beg Your Ladyship not to interfere in it, nor to oppose me further. If you do, you will have to answer for it to the King. You are under arrest. It will be no good to raise an uproar or to make a scene. I have sent word that I will bring you to the palace by tomorrow evening. We will have to hasten, but I will do my best to see that Your Ladyship travels as comfortably as may be."

She said no more in answer. But her manner by no means looked like giving in.

Giles was therefore on his guard. And when the gate swung open again, he was quick to get back to it ahead of her. This time there were two nuns standing in the archway.

"Mother Abbess," said he, addressing the older one, "I crave your pardon for calling you from your prayers. But I do assure you I am forced to. I have to take this lady to the capital at once and I need your aid."

Barbara made a step forward into the light of the lantern. The Abbess's keen eyes looked at her searchingly. Perhaps it was some resemblance to her mother, or the look of annoyance on her face, that made the Abbess pause a moment before she answered.

"But does—er—does she wish to go with you?" she asked presently.

"No, I do not," said Barbara sharply.

"I am sorry," said Giles. "But the lady's wishes on that point cannot be considered."

"And why not, pray?" the Abbess demanded quickly. "What authority have you to take her about the country against her will?"

"The King's authority," said Giles. "I am an officer in His Majesty's household. I carry with me letters of royal

warrant, should you wish to see them. If need be, I can command you to render me aid in the King's service. But this, I am sure, knowing the loyalty of your Order, will not be necessary. I want a coach with a good team of horses, a driver, and a woman to act as maid to this lady. All with the greatest possible speed, madam, if you please."

The larger abbeys and nunneries in those days were very important places, often almost like small townships within themselves, with farms, many servants, workers, and everything needful for the upkeep of life. And Giles knew well that the Abbess of Saint Bridget's could, just by a word of command, provide him with all he had asked for. It would be very awkward however, on account of time, if she should refuse him. The heads of big religious houses were sometimes very independent and had more than once in history shown defiance to the Crown. He was therefore watching her with eager impatience while she thought a moment before answering.

"What is your name?" she asked at length.

"Sir Giles Waggonwright, the King's Finder," said he.

Again the Abbess glanced at Barbara; then her sharp but kindly eyes searched this young man's face in the lantern's wavering glow. Through many years she had grown skillful in judging people by their looks.

"Reverend Mother," said Giles earnestly, "I beg of you, do not deny me. It will only mean I must seek help at the nearest military post and take this young lady away from you under armed guard. She must be at the palace by sunset tomorrow. I pledge you my word no harm shall come to her."

It seemed the Abbess found nothing to distrust in the determined face of the King's Finder. For suddenly with a gracious smile she stepped forward and took Barbara by the arm.

"It looks as if you would have to go, my dear," she said gently. "I will send Sister Monica, as well as my own niece, to keep you company. The gardener's wife will act as your maid. Do not forget that if you wish to visit us again, we shall be glad to see you at Saint Bridget's."

She turned. On her way in she gave some orders to the nun at her side, who at once hastened ahead of her.

Soon more lanterns began to appear. In their dim light figures gathered, whispered, and hurried to and fro. The other half of the big door was swung back. Hooves stamped. Chains jingled. From a stable on the left side of the courtyard, a pair of horses were led out onto the cobbled paving. Then a coach was pulled into position, facing the open gates. The horses were backed in and harnessed. A driver with a whip in his hand climbed to the seat. The Abbess appeared again with the heavily cloaked figures of three women following her. She beckoned Barbara into the yard, opening the coach door herself. With no sign of anger or resistance left in her, the Countess came obediently forward. She smiled a farewell to the Abbess and stepped into the carriage. Mollie jumped in and took a seat beside her. The three women followed and the door closed.

Outside on the lawn the King's Finder mounted his horse with a deep sigh of relief. And as the coach rattled out through the gate, he touched Midnight on the neck and fell in behind.

CHAPTER THIRTEEN

THE WATCHERS ON THE TERRACE

In a quiet corner of the castle terrace, Luke was seated on a stone bench. He was looking out across the country spread below, and particularly at the long white lines of roads that ran out farther than a man could see. Every once in a while he would spring forward to the parapet, peering with screwed-up eyes, as though to make something out. But always, disappointed, he returned to his seat.

Presently he heard footsteps running along the terrace and Anne arrived.

"Well, have you seen him yet?" she cried breathlessly.

"Seen who?" grunted Luke.

"Giles, of course."

"Oh, gracious, no!" said he, shaking his head with a frown of annoyance. "It's much too early to expect him yet. It's barely three o'clock."

"Then why are you sitting here?" asked Anne.

"Oh, I just came down to—er—to—"

"You came here to watch for Giles," said she, sitting on the bench beside him. "And don't you try to deny it."

"And why did you come here?" asked Luke, still looking out over the landscape.

"I came to tell you about the cat. I'm sure he's Agnes's."

"Why?"

"Listen," said she, lowering her voice. "He helped me make a fire just now. I thought the Countess might like one in her room when she gets back. And as we are not letting the servants into her apartments for the present, I got some wood and kindling and started to build it myself. And suddenly the cat appeared at my elbow and began handing me the sticks, in its mouth, the same as I saw him do in the Applewoman's hut long ago. He's Agnes's sure enough— Oh, look, is that horses coming, way over there on the middle road?"

Luke peered into the distance.

"No," said he presently. "Only the dust blowing up from the highway. I've been fooled by that a dozen times already. That's the four corners by Gerard's Mill. It's always windy there. How is the King now?"

"The surgeon is still with him," Anne answered. "And you'd never guess who the surgeon is: It's that old Dr. Seymour from our town, you remember? It seems he has become very famous since. But how on earth do you suppose the King came by such an accident, Luke? They say he stumbled and fell. Yet if he has not regained his senses since they picked him up, I don't see how they know. Maybe someone hit him or something. Who was the first to find him?"

"The Count Godfrey," said Luke. "He, at all events, is sure it was an accident. It seems he was on his way up to the royal apartments when he found the King lying at the foot of the tower stairs. He called me down to help. It looked like a badly sprained back to us—with a bump on his temple where his head had struck the stone steps. No bones broken. No signs of a struggle."

"Couldn't the bump have been made by somebody hitting him?" asked Anne. "Oh, I wish Giles were here!"

"So do I," said Luke. "But he couldn't help the King in this. Giles is no surgeon."

"I wish he were here, just the same," said Anne. "He might be able to find the man who did it. *I* am by no means sure the King wasn't struck down by some enemies. Maybe the same people had something to do with the Countess's disappearance too."

"Oh, how you talk!" cried Luke irritably. "I told you the message Giles gave me to bring: There was no kidnapping. Barbara is safe and sound. Why suspect anyone? It wasn't half an hour after I had carried the message to the King that Count Godfrey called to me. It must have been an accident—a natural one too. His Majesty hadn't eaten anything since Barbara went. You've seen him yourself—as pale as a ghost. Well, a sudden fit of faintness as he was coming down those dizzy winding stairs, he stumbles, and there you have it."

"Was he very glad to get Giles's message?" asked Anne.

"Um—er—yes," said Luke, frowning. "He was overjoyed to hear no harm had come to her. Then he asked no end of questions, trying to learn more from me. But I could tell him nothing further—merely that your brother had galloped off into the night after giving me those few words—which I had brought to him in nine hours of the fastest riding a man ever did."

"Yes, you certainly wasted no time, to get here so early," said Anne.

"When the King found that I had no further news," Luke went on, "he grew very solemn and thoughtful. He seemed to be puzzling over something."

"Maybe," said Anne slowly, "he was wondering why Barbara *went* away—since she wasn't carried away."

"What do you mean?" asked Luke sharply.

"Oh, look!" cried Anne, again rushing to the parapet. "See, over there, on the other road. Can that be Giles now?"

"No, it isn't," snapped Luke. "It's a herd of cattle. Do stop jumping about!"

"Oh, I wish he'd come!" Anne sighed, sinking back on the seat. "You do think he will, don't you, Luke? There are robbers on those roads, you know."

"Of course he'll come," said Luke. "He's able to take care of himself—and Barbara too. Don't worry. Tell me: What did Dr. Seymour say when he last came from the King's room?"

"Oh, a whole lot about *vertebrains*—or something," said Anne. "He is not worried over the lump on the temple. It's the back, he says, will give the most trouble. Badly wrenched—perhaps injured for life. I don't think much of that old physic-monger. He does a powerful lot of talking, but he doesn't *do* anything. And the King is still unconscious. Neither does the Queen Mother, I fancy, place much faith in Seymour. Poor lady! She's beside herself with worry."

"Have all the guests gone yet?" asked Luke.

"Almost all," said Anne. "They have had some sore hurrying to do, to get packed and everything. It was feared that some of them might take offense at being asked to depart at such short notice. But the Queen Mother went around to each one and explained that the King's accident had put off the wedding—she could not say for how long. She told them that Dr. Seymour had asked for absolute quiet in and around the castle. I must say they all behaved extremely well, expressed their deep regrets and went off as quietly as they could."

"Well, you for one are glad that's over, I'll wager," said Luke.

"I am indeed," said Anne. "I was so terrified that some of them would get to know the Countess wasn't here and start some sort of a scandal story going. That was another funny thing I never told you about that cat. Yesterday I left Barbara's rooms and forgot to lock the door behind me. While I was away, one of the guests— a duchess, I believe, she was—took a notion to call on the Countess. It seemed she knocked and, getting no answer, had half opened the door to walk in. Anyway, I arrived back just in time to see the big cat attacking the Duchess, spitting at her and driving her away. And you remember what a friendly creature he is ordinarily— even playing with the spaniel. What do you make of that?"

"Well, nothing much out of the way," grunted Luke. "The cat likes spaniels, it seems, and doesn't like duchesses. Very natural— Oh, there's somebody beckoning from the door. One of the Queen's ladies. It will be for you, Anne."

"Goodness!" whispered Anne, springing up. "I hope it's not bad news about the King."

"If it is," Luke called after her, "come back and let me know as soon as you can get away. I'll be here."

As a matter of fact, it was bad news. The King was worse. But even if Anne had come back to bring it, she would not have found Luke upon the terrace.

For shortly after she had left, those watching eyes of the esquire had spied at last the tiny shape of a coach, away off in the distance, lumbering toward the castle.

In a dozen breakneck bounds he went flying down the garden steps. At the foot, within a small clump of trees, he had a horse tied, saddled and waiting.

A moment later he was galloping down the road to meet his master.

CHAPTER FOURTEEN

THE RETURN OF THE FINDER

Giles had hardly spoken to Barbara since they had left the convent—no more than a polite word or two at the places where he had halted to change horses or get food for his passengers.

Now, from afar, he was glad to see the figure of Luke galloping toward him. He was glad, too, to have the old castle loom at last in sight. It meant the end of a hard and anxious journey. But somehow coming back to it this evening was not the same. Usually this ancient home of kingship, with its weather-beaten battlements rising up and up against the sky like the fingers of majesty itself, used, without fail, to thrill him every time he saw it. He was a part of it, fitted into its power and being—just as the castle itself fitted so perfectly around the top of the sharply pointed hill it stood on.

Tired and travel worn he was; but at this moment he did not, he felt, want to sleep in it tonight. He would go off again at once, he told himself. As soon as he had handed Barbara over, he would ask for leave to go upon his holiday. What mattered his weariness? He would take the trip home in easy stages and rest up on the way. He would not linger at the palace of the King.

As soon as Luke joined up with him, falling in behind the coach and riding at his side, he told these plans to his esquire.

"Giles, you can't do it," whispered Luke when he had ended. "Of course the King will give you leave if you wish to go. Certainly he has always been more friend than master—to both of us. But he will think it strange of you, your wanting to leave him again right away— even if he doesn't speak of it. Especially now, when he is not well, as I told you."

Giles said nothing.

"Besides that, we need you, the Queen Mother above all. She has had to arrange everything, with no one to share authority or to give advice. She is nearly crazed with fear."

"With fear?" asked Giles. "What of?"

"Oh, things are at a dreadful pass up there! The King fell and hurt himself. They have a surgeon with him. Nobody knows what's going to happen."

"You mean—" Giles hesitated and his expression changed queerly. It was almost as if he were trying to beat back some dreadful guilty thing rising in his thoughts. "You mean there is danger? That the King may—*may die?*"

"No one knows," said Luke. "But stay, I beg you, tonight at least—if only for the Queen Mother's sake."

Again Giles made no answer. And Luke persuaded him no further. They rode on up to the castle.

Here no noisy welcome awaited the King's Finder returning with the King's bride. Instead a solemn hush of anxious fear seemed hanging over the whole palace. Luke directed the driver around to a private entrance to the King's tower. There Giles got Barbara quietly out of the coach and at once led her up the winding stair. The esquire followed.

In the antechamber to the King's bedroom, they found three persons: the Queen Mother, Anne, and Dr. Seymour. The faces of all were very grave. The Queen barely glanced at them. Seymour was the first to speak.

"I fear there is very little hope for His Majesty's recovery. He has not once regained his senses since he fell. It is the spine, badly hurt—very badly. The pulse is so weak now, it can hardly be felt. It is my sad duty to tell Your Majesty"—he turned, bowing, to the Queen— "that the end can only be a matter of a few hours— perhaps a few minutes."

Giles came over to the poor mother sitting huddled in a chair.

"Will Your Majesty give me leave to go in and see him?" he whispered.

The Queen nodded without looking up. Giles turned the handle softly and passed into the bedroom.

A dim light came though half-drawn curtains. In a

raised alcove, on the bed, the body of the King lay very still. Coming nearer, Giles could see the face was twisted in pain; but the chest did not seem to move. It looked almost as though breathing had stopped already. He leaned over and spoke into his friend's ear softly. There was no answering sign.

Tears came suddenly into his own eyes. He turned away and moved to the open door.

The awful waiting stillness was only disturbed by the gentle sobbing of the Queen's prayers. But Giles did not hear it. He stood there on the threshold between the two rooms, hearing nothing, seeing nothing. It was as if all the world and all his senses were blotted out. Only one thing kept pounding in his head, over and over: His friend, the greatest friend he had ever had, was dying. Not even finding that the success of his faithful quest had come too late, not even knowing that the bride he brought back could never be the King's, nothing had power to hold his mind now but the picture of that stricken man upon the bed behind him. His friend was dying.

And then there came a gentle knock on the stair door. Swiftly Luke tiptoed across the room and opened it.

An old woman stood in the archway peering in, two enormous black cats at her feet.

"May I see the King?" was all she said.

"*Agnes!*" gasped Anne, springing forward.

The Queen stopped praying and raised her head.

"Your Majesty," snapped Dr. Seymour, "I beg you do not allow that woman in here. That is Shragga the Witch."

At this the two cats suddenly raised their backs and hissed.

"She is a dangerous sorceress," he went on. "Please do not let her see the King. She is from my town. I know her."

"Yes," said Agnes, coming forward, fixing him with an angry eye. "You know me. And I know you. For it was you, for years, who set the magistrates on me, with your tales of Devil tricks, hounding me from place to place, forcing me to hide like a rat. You'd have had me burned if you could. And why? Because you knew I was a better doctor than you could ever be, you pompous, blowing bag of bombast! You never knew enough anatomy to cure a baby of the colic. And now you with your great learning would keep me from the King, would you? We shall see."

Suddenly she turned from him to the Queen Mother.

"He calls me a witch, my lady." She swept a pointing finger around the other persons in the room. "Well, ask *them* what I am."

But Luke was already on his knees at the Queen's chair.

"I implore Your Majesty," he said. "Do not hold her from your son. She is a great physician. I was a cripple once, dragging on crutches, and she cured me. Please, *please*, madam, let her go in."

The Queen looked from his earnest face across to Giles.

"It is true, every word," said the King's Finder. "Believe him, Your Majesty, and let her do what she can. Minutes are precious now."

Dr. Seymour bustled forward, opening his mouth to say something. But the Queen had risen from her chair. She held a hand up to silence him.

"Enough!" she said gently. "The woman shall go in."

Alone Agnes passed into the King's bedroom. And as she closed the door behind her, Dr. Seymour took his wallet from a table and sneaked quietly down the stairs.

CHAPTER FIFTEEN

The King Pays a Debt

An hour passed, or so it seemed to those who waited in the antechamber. For the Queen Mother's sake all tried to hide, under a show of calm patience, their eagerness for news, for the answer to that dread question: Had Agnes come in time to save the King?

It was Anne, sitting nearest to the bedroom door, who first broke the silence. She ran quickly to the Queen.

"Madam, I hear voices. The King must be awake."

"The Saints be thanked—and the good woman too," sighed the Queen.

At that moment the door opened and Agnes's head popped out.

"His Majesty wishes to see the Countess," she said and disappeared again.

Barbara rose at once and hurried in. She ran quickly across the room and knelt sobbing by the King's bed. Agnes closed the door gently and waited by it.

The King feebly raised his hand and laid it on the girl's golden head.

"There, there!" he whispered. "I know. I know."

"Oh, I didn't mean to hurt you," she cried. "Thank Heaven you are better! It would have killed me had you died. I couldn't help it. When you asked me to marry you, it was different. I liked you, as you well know. My father and all of them told me it was my duty, if you wanted me, to be your queen—to make you happy. And I thought I could—then."

"I know," the King repeated. "I knew when Luke brought me word that you were not carried off. I was sure then that you must have gone of your own accord and, most likely, because you loved someone else more than myself."

"It was so stupid and unfair of me," said Barbara. "I should have come and told you outright, instead of running like a coward. But I only began to find it out after our betrothal—one day when I was at the lake and he helped me get flowers for the Queen Mother. I suppose they call it falling in love. But after that day I grew more and more certain it would be wrong to marry you while I loved Sir Giles. Then the preparations for the wedding began, kings and princes coming, and the news sent out all over the world. The thought of humbling you in the eyes of everyone, coming to you begging to be freed of the pledge I'd given, seemed impossible. And so, like a fool, I still said nothing, hoping to go through with what I had begun. But that last night, the night before the wedding, I saw at last clearly that there was a lifetime of unhappiness ahead of both of us if I married you. So I just ran away. I thought if I went into a convent and took the veil, then at least no one could say I had deserted the King for one of his subjects. You would be spared that much. Tell me, tell me you forgive me!"

The King smiled.

"Do not blame yourself. It was my fault too. From the start I guessed you did not love me in the way that I did you. And rather than face the matter honestly in my own heart, I tried to fool myself. Mercifully the knowledge came slowly to me. . . . I feel much better now, thanks to that old woman there. I'll soon be up and busy. Tell her to bring Giles to me."

A moment later Giles came in alone.

"Your Majesty, Agnes bids me warn you that you must not talk longer now. You should sleep."

"There is not much left to say," the King whispered. "She loves you. And I am glad that it is you, and no one else, who takes her from me. You saved my life once, Giles, and I told you that I would not forget. I pay the debt now—in full. Go with him, Barbara. But after you are married, he remains, please, in my service. I cannot afford to lose my two best friends at once. Good luck to you! Good-bye—till tomorrow."

The Queen Mother entered as they went out.

Silently Giles and Barbara walked across to the head

of the stairs. There they stopped, gazing at each other through a golden haze of wonder, love, and happiness. And, of a sudden, for the first time they kissed.

Presently they heard Luke moving fidgetily by the window. They had forgotten for the moment that this world held anyone else but themselves.

"Where is Agnes?" asked Anne, jumping up.

The Applewoman was nowhere in the room. Yet they had all seen her leave the King.

Giles, still a little crazy with happiness, grabbed Barbara by the hand and dragged her wildly down the stairs to look for Agnes.

Luke and Anne followed. There were a thousand questions they all wanted to ask her: Where she had been all these years; how she knew the King was sick; how the cat came to the Countess's apartments; how the shell got into the pocket of the tunic. And no end more.

Around and around and down the dizzy winding stairs they went, gabbling like a lot of children out of school.

But at the bottom they found the courtyard empty under the silent stars.

Agnes was gone.

About the Author

Hugh Lofting was born in England in 1886 and studied engineering in London and at the Massachusetts Institute of Technology. He settled in the United States after his marriage in 1912.

During World War I he was commissioned a lieutenant in the Irish Guards. Distressed by the suffering inflicted on animals by the war, he took up writing illustrated letters to his children, and these eventually became *The Story of Doctor Dolittle*.

Hugh Lofting went on to write many books for children, including *The Voyages of Doctor Dolittle*, which won the Newbery Medal in 1923.

About the Illustrator

Tatsuro Kiuchi was born in Japan and studied art at the Art Center College of Design in Pasadena, California. He received a bronze medal from the Society of Illustrators in 1991. He lives in Tokyo.